The Unquiet Sleep

by William Haggard
author of *The Arena*

WILLIAM HAGGARD's talent for writing about the ethical and sometimes criminal lapses of a few members of the higher echelons of business and the Establishment is never better displayed than in this suspense-filled novel of international smuggling and narcotics.

Actually the product in question was not considered a narcotic. Its respectable manufacturer called it "Mecron," and the less reverent referred to it as the "Executive's Friend." You took the tranquilizer, lay down for an hour and got up ready to make a fresh start on an evening of fun or work. But one day a research chemist found he had made a demented addict of a monkey with these pills, and other

(Continued on back flap)

DATE DUE

Feb 7 '74			
Jul 28 '75			
JUN 2 1980	NOV — 1		
AUG 1 2 1980			
MAR 1 1983			
JUL 1 5 1983			
DEC 2 7 1984			
NOV 2 9 1986			
OCT 2 4 1987			
DEC — 1 1987			
NOV 1 6 1988			
NOV 2 9 1988			
MAR 1 5 1989			

GAYLORD   PRINTED IN U.S.A.

BURLINGAME PUBLIC LIBRARY
Burlingame, California

1. UNLESS OTHERWISE DESIGNATED, books may be kept for two weeks and may be renewed once for the same length of time.

2. Overdue fees will be levied on all magazines, books, and phonograph record albums according to the schedule posted at the main desk.

3. DAMAGES AND LOSSES of Library-owned property will be paid for by the borrower.

4. RESPONSIBILITY for all books taken on his card rests with the borrower as well as for all fees accruing to his card. Notification of loss of card does not free the borrower of his responsibility.

The Unquiet Sleep

THE UNQUIET SLEEP

WILLIAM HAGGARD

IVES WASHBURN, INC.

NEW YORK   1962

CHAPTER

1

THE MINISTRY OF Social Welfare was decidedly an odd one. It wasn't Pensions and National Insurance, and it wasn't Health; it wasn't Housing and Local Government, and it wasn't Labour. All these strange animals were necessary ingredients in keeping any contemporary government in power, but the departments concerned had Ministers already, Ministers and attendant satellites who would bitterly have resented, even more bitterly fought, any suggestion that their importance be diminished. So that Social Welfare didn't in practice do much for welfare. But though not a big ministry that didn't mean that it wasn't an important one. On the contrary it was vital, for Social Welfare was in fact a euphemism for public relations. The real business of Social Welfare was to keep the administration respectable; to plant the image of a socially conscious benevolence; to foster the frail plant; to harvest it. Defeats were represented as deliberate and planned advances, routs as concessions. Her Majesty's Opposition writhed but were helpless. There was irony in this, since Social Welfare had been one of their own creations when in office. They hadn't foreseen that in a year or two it would become the private instrument of a Prime Minister whom they regarded, at any rate in public where they had to, as a clever reactionary. Hearing them discuss him you could almost smell the brimstone.

And something else as well, and it was fear. The Prime Minister was a reactionary—all his party were reactionaries—but this was by definition. But he was also a very shrewd man, and that was, by reluctant admission, something much more serious. He had been clever about Welfare, for example, very clever indeed, for he had sent there as Minister Mr. Robert Seneschal, thereby both emasculating his own most danger-

I

ous rival, since no politician could be really dangerous without one of the few great departments of state behind him, and at the same time providing at Social Welfare the perfect figurehead. For Robert Seneschal had already an established aura, a public image wholly acceptable; he was a liberal, defining that term as somebody who wouldn't viciously object to social changes but·who wouldn't wish to be too beastly to those who suffered as their result. The Prime Minister thought him ineffective, but he hadn't a doubt about his position in the party. Robert Seneschal was necessary to the party: it could hardly have won an election without him. Indeed if it hadn't been for a miscalculation of the temper of the backbenchers on a matter where they, but not Robert Seneschal, smelt national prestige, Mr. Seneschal would have been Prime Minister himself. This the Prime Minister knew. So Robert Seneschal found himself not, as he had hoped and indeed deserved, at the Home Office, but stuck with Social Welfare and a hatful of bull to the effect that he alone could handle it. He was too experienced openly to complain, but he bided his time. Sooner or later the Prime Minister would slip from his elegant tightrope: Seneschal told himself that sooner or later it was inevitable. The trouble was that so far he had been remarkably sure-footed, and meanwhile the heir apparent wasn't getting any younger. Long reigns were notoriously hard on princes.

Nevertheless at Social Welfare Seneschal worked well, for he knew that a reputation as a disgruntled man was immediately fatal. Moreover he was able, and he enjoyed his own ability. He had been particularly skilful in his choice of Parliamentary Secretary.

His name was Henry Leggatt, and Seneschal had personally advanced his case with the Prime Minister. Not that it had needed much advancing, since Henry Leggatt had perfect qualifications for the post of second image. For the party had discovered that nowadays two were necessary. Mr. Seneschal was one of them—liberal, ex-academic, wholly reliable in such matters as prison reform and the divorce laws. Reform— but of course! But not too much and not too quickly. One mustn't upset the prison officers, and certainly not the bishops.

But that wasn't quite enough when the party, the Prime Minister especially, was conscious that it struggled with a certain reputation. Too many people to be politically convenient thought of it as a sort of club still, one which you joined by birth not brains. And that cost votes. But Henry Leggatt was ideal to give the apparent lie to it. He was what the inner ring, though never openly, would have called a self-made man. They supposed he had been to school somewhere, but they didn't remember where, since wherever it had been it hadn't been one of their own establishments. He was able in his unassuming way and he had an excellent war record. Not in one of their own regiments, but an undeniably gallant record. Henry Leggatt could be presented as the party's New Man, as proof that it was now wide open, welcoming fresh talent, welcoming the Henry Leggatts.

All three or four of them.

Moreover Henry Leggatt could talk, and well; he was a natural. He was that rarest of blends, effective in public, good in the House. Over the air you sensed sincerity, and on telly you saw it in reassuringly solid flesh. Robert Seneschal privately thought him a little dull, for Robert Seneschal had won a First at Oxford, and Leggatt had at bottom been a salesman. A very good one, no doubt—remarkably successful. Hassertons had put him on the board as sales director, and Hassertons was one of the first three pharmaceutical houses in the country. He must, Robert Seneschal decided, be feeling the financial draught a bit. As a private Member he would have been all right; he could have kept his directorship and most of his perks as well, but as a junior Minister on a Parliamentary Secretary's shameful and shameless pittance he could hardly but be pushed.

Or rather his wife would be pushed. Robert Seneschal frowned, for he had never admired Patricia Leggatt. He knew a good deal about her, for she was the wife of a subordinate. She was well-connected where in politics it mattered. Seneschal shivered for he had himself married money. A politician was

3

obliged to marry carefully if he meant to get anywhere, or rather a politician was obliged to if he belonged to Mr. Seneschal's party. Not that Patricia was rich. She had connection not money—only a modest private income—and Seneschal didn't suppose that any part of it went into the housekeeping. Patricia Leggatt would have other things to do with her money than help a husband in a difficulty.

Robert Seneschal sat down at his desk. He had other things to do himself, the routine of a ministry which, if it wasn't one of the great ones, was at least extremely busy. He had papers to read and he began to do so. He smiled his Common Room smile. Henry Leggatt would have papers too. Across the corridor Henry Leggatt would be reading papers. But he wouldn't be understanding them.

Across the corridor Henry Leggatt was reading papers and he was understanding them very well. Not in Seneschal's sense, for Seneschal had what was called in Whitehall a first-class brain, and Leggatt neither possessed this gift nor wished to. It was his instinct that a Minister's business wasn't to understand his papers—not in detail, not in the way his civil servants did: instead it was to think politically, to sense complications, public opinion, trouble; to smell the sharp wind of a world where administrative convenience were very dirty words.

It was an opinion shared in quarters which would have surprised him if he had known of them. His Permanent Secretary, for instance, held it. His Permanent Secretary too had a first-class brain, so effortlessly first class that he mistrusted others. He mistrusted in particular the first-class academic brain of Mr. Robert Seneschal. That sort of thing was for fellow civil servants. In Ministers it was a nuisance.

It was the Permanent Secretary's amiable habit to wait for one of Seneschal's absences before he put up papers on which he wanted a clear-cut decision. Mr. Seneschal would minute papers back again; he would ask questions, prevaricate. But Henry Leggatt would decide. Not always rightly, but any man

4

who was right even fifty-one per cent of the time was beating the human average, and Henry Leggatt batted better than fifty-one. Or so his Permanent Secretary considered. So he waited till Mr. Seneschal was away before he put forward anything which he thought important but not so important that it would have to go to Cabinet in any case. He always got an answer and mostly the answer he wanted.

It was a well-run ministry, beautifully effective, for the Permanent Secretary was a good one. Moreover he liked Leggatt personally. The fact that he wasn't brilliant didn't disturb a man who was. The Permanent Secretary preferred it that way. Leggatt had something which he respected. It was integrity. It was a word which the rack wouldn't have choked from him in public, but in private its overtones did not disturb him. In any case he thought it the right one.

Henry Leggatt worked steadily till half-past twelve, when his private secretary came in quietly. Peter Davis was a serious young man—very serious indeed, even for an Assistant Principal. His private politics were intellectual left, and this the Permanent Secretary had known when he had agreed to his appointment as a Minister's copyboy. He hadn't been worried at all. Peter Davis was intelligent; Peter Davis would go far in the service. By the time he was forty his politics would be those of every other civil servant, a faintly sardonic determination to keep your Minister, whatever his political complexion, from doing anything really stupid. Short of the really stupid you were helpless. But that was accepted.

Peter Davis said now: 'Your wife has arrived, sir.'

'Good Lord, I'd forgotten.'

It was true, Leggatt thought—true and regrettable. He had got himself stuck in again. They hadn't been seeing much of each other lately: he'd been working too hard, neglecting her. Or rather, he decided, she could say she was being neglected.

He put the thought aside, for it wasn't the moment for it. He wasn't normally afraid of facing facts, and where his marriage was concerned a long cool look was overdue. But

5

this wasn't the moment for it. He'd asked his wife to lunch and she'd accepted.

'Show her straight in, please. I'll go and wash.'

Peter Davis came back with Patricia Leggatt. He was an observant young man as well as serious, and he had quickly acquired the perfect manner for a Minister's private secretary. In a Minister's own room a private secretary, a very young one, had to be something more than an official. In a sense he was a sort of servant—must be to do the job properly. Peter Davis said politely, half butler, half host: 'Would you care for a glass of sherry?'

'Isn't there any gin?'

'Not here, I'm afraid. I'll get some, though.'

Peter Davis went away for the gin. He hadn't liked it. He had met the Minister's wife before, and he was thinking that that was Patricia Leggatt all over. Aloof, more than a little arrogant, though heaven knew she wouldn't realize it. In his personal and private shorthand Peter Davis had tagged Patricia Leggatt, and the tag was upper arty. It had amused him to imagine her background, for the Minister's modest flat where he had met her clearly wasn't her natural stamping ground. That would be somewhere in the Cadogans, he had decided, somewhere rich and talkative. The people lived by taking each other's photographs. Not really, of course: they all had private incomes which it was very bad form to mention; they all assumed that you had too. And they talked—how they talked! They talked novels and pictures and plays, and operas you'd never heard of. Not that they knew much about them, for solid knowledge meant work —hard reading and even thought. But they knew what was new.

What was new was worth chattering about.

Peter Davis walked down the corridor, his footfall silent on the plushy carpeting, pushing open the swing door which led into the common world of ordinary civil servants. Here there was a horrid stone: his steel-tipped heels rang sharply. He found a colleague who he knew kept gin—it was against the rules but Establishments were reasonable. He put it on a tray, with glasses, returning to his master's room. Henry Leggatt and Patricia were standing, Henry helping her into an expensive fur.

'I've brought some gin.'

'I'm afraid we must be going.' Patricia Leggatt smiled her brief cool smile again, and again Peter Davis didn't like it. He was a sort of servant perhaps, but not that sort of servant. He went to the door, opening it, watching them down the corridor. He thought Henry Leggatt was walking too heavily. Patricia's clear voice came back to him.

'Have you fixed that hotel yet? Cortina is going to be crowded. It always is at Christmas.'

Davis didn't catch Leggatt's answer but he caught his tone. It had been almost deprecatory, and for a moment Peter Davis felt resentment. His Minister's politics were his own private poison, but he admired him as a man. He was a considerate master; he never changed his mind and then said you had; he never let you down. Peter Davis didn't like to hear him apologizing. About money, he guessed—not being able to afford something.

Peter Davis wasn't particularly experienced with women but he knew something important about marriage. There was a variety of ways in which a man could treat his wife and still live happily. But he mustn't apologize; he mustn't feel *required* to.

Peter Davis went back to his little room, but he didn't begin to work again. Instead he sat frowning, considering Patricia Leggatt. He neither liked nor trusted her. He was a serious young man to the point of being something of a prig. Patricia Leggatt was the wife of a Minister. She shouldn't be going to night clubs, or not with another man. Alone with him.

Peter Davis went to a night club perhaps twice a year, and always with his brother. Ron Davis was a biochemist. He worked for Cameron and Cole—pharmaceuticals of the highest class, the equals and rivals of Hassertons. He had enough money for his needs and no politics whatsoever; he was attractive to women when he wished to be, and he adored his work. It had never occurred to him that when he died he would do otherwise than walk into oblivion. He was a happy man.

And just occasionally he fancied what he called a fling, and when he did he would take his brother to a fashionable night club. They had gone to the Green Baytree, and Ron Davis had settled to the simple pleasure of watching its clients. He had pointed uninhibitedly.

'Smashing piece.'

Behind the dark glasses, wholly unnecessary, it had been Patricia Leggatt. Ron Davis had begun to elaborate. . . . She wasn't flaunting too much of a good thing—he hadn't himself gone transatlantic—but she had everything where it ought to be. Pretty affair to sit on, slung nice and high. Lovely body in fact. He liked her hair-do too—bold bang of well-brushed hair across one eye. It mightn't be fashionable, but it was a style which had never been improved on for a woman with that sort of face. Fine-featured, a little long. Patrician. Wow.

Peter Davis said absently: 'Yes.' Too absently, for his brother pounced at once.

'You know her?'

'Oh yes.'

'Then introduce me.'

'No.'

'Why not? Who is she?'

'She's my Minister's wife.'

Ron Davis was silent, eating and drinking with appetite. The food was unspeakable but the champagne authentic. Presently he said thoughtfully: 'Henry Leggatt's wife? He was in Hassertons, wasn't he? Sales director.'

'He had to give that up of course.'

'He hasn't a connection still?'

'No *direct* connection.' Peter Davis was being cautious.

'He couldn't go back to them?'

'Only if he resigned.'

'D'you think he's ever thought of it?'

Peter Davis had frowned again. He was fond of his brother, but it was stupid to pretend that delicacy was his strong point.

8

Besides, the question was an awkward one, for Peter had wondered himself. A director's chair in Hassertons must have been worth a good deal more money than a Parliamentary Secretary would ever see, and money. . . .

Clearly Patricia liked it. She liked it very much.

But Ron had changed the subject, pointing again at Patricia Leggatt's partner. They were dancing very close.

'Do you know the man too?'

Peter Davis shook his head.

'He might be a Greek—of a sort.'

It was an accurate observation. Patricia Leggatt's partner had thick dark hair, a little but quite naturally curling, rather lower on his forehead, denser on the nape of his neck than most men's. His eyelids were cut beautifully. His nose was firm, high-bridged, but somehow faintly blurred. The forehead was marmoreal. You might have seen him in stone in the Campidoglio if someone with a handful of plasticine and a taste for decadence had been at work there. Except that he was alive—very alive indeed. He smiled a lot and he danced quite beautifully. And very close to Patricia Leggatt.

She didn't seem to be objecting.

Later, in the taxi to their flat, Ron Davis had returned to Henry Leggatt.

'You said he might go back to Hassertons?'

'I said perhaps he could. And it's a big perhaps.'

'It mightn't be a bad idea.'

'What on earth do you mean?'

'Oh, nothing. Sorry.' The taxi stopped and Ron had paid it.

It had been an enjoyable evening, but now, sitting at his desk again, Peter Davis wasn't enjoying himself. He was worried and would have admitted it. But there was nothing he could do. The wise civil servant minded his own business, the wise private secretary to a junior Minister especially. Just the same he liked the man. But his wife, Patricia Leggatt. . . .

Peter Davis sighed. It might have been more manageable if Leggatt hadn't been still in love with her. For that was obvious, a discreet little joke for the discreetest of company.

9

He looked at her like—oh, like Ron Davis had, though much less frankly. Ron Davis would have known about Patricia Leggatt.

It seemed her husband didn't.

Ron Davis went through the laboratory, out into the annexe, walking down the long line of cages. He wasn't quite at ease, since he hadn't any business to be experimenting with Mecron. He worked for Cameron and Cole, whereas Mecron was something of Hassertons', something new which they were pushing hard. It was effective too—no doubt about it; it released you almost at once, and it didn't destroy your evening. Take Mecron, lie down for a bit, and in an hour you felt wonderful.

Ron Davis knew, for he had taken it himself. He had taken it five, six times—he couldn't remember—and then one evening he had found himself thinking of Mecron. He had thought of it hard—too hard. He was a chemist and he had been frightened. He had turned to the whisky instead.

Now he walked down the long line of cages till he came to Ermyntrude. Ermyntrude was a monkey and Ron Davis had grown fond of her. He was ashamed of what he was doing. He was feeding her Mecron. He'd been feeding her Mecron for three months.

He stopped before the cage, more shocked than he could remember. It had been worsening for some time, but this morning it was intolerable. As she saw him she almost screamed; she scrabbled the wire meshing of the cage, dancing obscenely, desperate. The simian, near-human gestures sickened him.

Ermyntrude was an addict.

He gave her her Mecron, turning away. He didn't want to watch her—it wouldn't be agreeable—but in forty-eight seconds by his stop watch Ermyntrude would be out.

He used them to walk back to the laboratory, filling a hypodermic, going back to the annexe grimly. He'd been attached to Ermyntrude, for once she had been a charmer.

He approached the cage quietly, for she mustn't see him. Nor the hypodermic. Ermyntrude had been intelligent once —once before he had destroyed her.

. . . Yes, she was out all right.

He killed her quickly, cursing.

2

COLONEL CHARLES RUSSELL sat in his untidy room in the Security Executive reading a report. On the face of it the report dealt with a matter which was nothing to do with him, since drugs weren't formally 'security'. Come to that, he was thinking, almost nothing was formally security and almost anything might be. Charles Russell saw some very queer paper indeed.

The report he was reading at the moment had been written by a senior official for another even more eminent, but whether a Minister would see it depended on the very distinguished official. It was Russell's guess that he would not, since the report was both alarming and indeterminate, and it was notorious that Ministers had a great distaste for being alarmed and one even greater for being made to feel helpless. When the two coincided some civil servant lost advancement.

Russell read on steadily, though the report told him much that he already knew. So far, in Britain, drugs hadn't been a major problem. The Narcotics Section of Scotland Yard was the smallest in the building, the Dangerous Drugs Branch at the Home Office ran on a man and a boy. True there was an official in Washington, experienced and level-headed, who sincerely believed that the trade in narcotics was part of a communist plot to corrupt the West—deliberately, even brilliantly organized to just that end. Russell didn't disbelieve him, he was too experienced to disbelieve things, but he had been trained to assess evidence, and this particular evidence, or most of it, he'd seen. It hadn't quite convinced him. There were holes in it, too many inferences. Russell had mentally marked it 'case but unproven'. In any event there wasn't any evidence of a politically motivated narcotics ring in Britain.

Nor was the writer saying that he had found one. He knew

the position as well as Russell—better, since it was his business professionally. What was worrying him was tranquillizers, and for a reason which Russell appreciated. For tranquillizers broke the established pattern, which was that drug-takers were either very rich or very poor. Criminal narcotics weren't, by and large, a middle-class habit. Tranquillizers might be, and that could raise quite new problems.

Russell walked to the window, staring into the courtyard. He had a horror of tranquillizers, one which he would have admitted was unprofessional. It verged on moral judgment, and for moral judgments he had a wholly professional mistrust. Offence was the word which came to him: tranquillizers offended him. . . . A man went to his office daily, flogging his guts out. And that was half his life. To lead the other half he needed drugs. Not narcotics perhaps, but drugs just the same. Pills. White pills or coloured, extravagantly packaged. He needed a pill to face his leisure.

Russell shook his head. When he wanted a let-down he drank sherry, and when he wanted a lift he knew to a fluid ounce precisely what spirits would do for him. Pills struck him as an abortion would: as something unnatural.

Nevertheless he went back to the report with misgiving. Tranquillizers were deplorable but they weren't unlawful; they weren't dangerous drugs and they certainly weren't poisons. You could buy them at chemists and some men did. Russell might mistrust, but there was nothing he could do.

But he read on doggedly, his expression slowly changing. For by now the report had stopped talking about tranquillizers and was discussing a particular tranquillizer. It was one called Mecron. So far the report had been a summary—the drug habit generally, its social and political overtones, almost its philosophy. But now it was talking about something called Mecron.

Russell stopped reading again, lighting a pipe deliberately. He turned the report over, looking at its back. As he had expected a sealed envelope was tagged to it. It was addressed to him personally and in a handwriting he recognized. Russell smiled, but he did not open the envelope. He never peeped.

13

That would have been bad discipline, and moreover it didn't pay. He returned to the report with a calm grim interest. Colonel Russell was smelling meat.

Mecron. It had certainly caught on. It had been advertised, of course—cleverly put over by the highly competent agency which Hassertons employed. And it did seem to work, and well. You took one when you came home from work; lay down for an hour; and presto, you could take your wife out. Or maybe do better. No hangover, no depression: you felt as good as new. The Executives' Friend, they called it—not Hassertons or the agency, they were much too sophisticated —but the phrase had stuck. The Executives' Friend, indeed! Russell shuddered but he went on reading.

And something seemed to have gone wrong with Mecron, something very awkward. It wasn't as though it were some wretched patent medicine; it was something put out by a respectable firm with the formula on the tube. It wasn't a dangerous drug and it clearly wasn't technically a poison. Nevertheless doctors had begun to worry about it. There had been several cases, nothing you could put your finger on, but all with people who'd been taking Mecron. Rather too wide a margin for coincidence, or so the doctors thought. But what could they do? Respectable doctors didn't push proprietary medicines, not even Hassertons', but they also had to be very careful about knocking them. They might have stopped pre-scribing Mecron, but its sales were up and up. That was queer, even ominous. It could hardly be the advertising alone.

Russell carefully opened the envelope at the back of the report.

All this is nothing to do with us, or not on the face of it. But one aspect might be, so I thought you should see it. Mecron is made by Hassertons, and a Mr. Henry Leggatt was one of their directors. At the moment he's Parliamentary Secretary in Social Welfare.

R.B.

R.B. stood for Rachel Borrodaile. She was one of Russell's assistants and a very shrewd woman.

14

Russell burnt the note, initialling the report without comment. He put it in his out-tray, smiling again. That was the hell of security but also its charm, its quite undeniable charm. Its frontiers ran nowhere: nothing was security and anything might be. Mecron was a proprietary drug, an increasingly successful one. Also it seemed to be suspect. There was nothing for Russell in that—nothing at all. Proprietary drugs weren't the business of the Security Executive, and Russell wouldn't have dreamt of interfering with the admirably conducted bodies whose pigeon they really were. But Mecron was made by Hassertons, and a Minister of the Crown had once been on Hassertons' board. Naturally he'd had to resign: if he still had shares they were probably with nominees. That was the usual form. If there was trouble he could plead that he hadn't a connection, but plead would be the word. They'd put him in the wrong at once, straight on the defensive, and Ministers didn't fancy being put on the defensive.

And nor did governments. The extension wasn't impossible if there was a serious scandal. There wasn't yet, but you could never tell.

Not in the Security Executive.

Henry Leggatt was very tired. He hadn't expected to enjoy an evening out; he had been working too hard and would have preferred an early bed, but Patricia had been insistent and his conscience wasn't clear. Being the wife of a busy Minister couldn't be amusing, especially when you were a good deal younger. Patricia Leggatt was twenty-nine, and Henry was conscious that he was forty-four.

Forty-four years. Tonight they seemed exceptionally long ones. He caught himself thinking that she hadn't exactly met him half-way. Dinner and a theatre might have been enough, but no, she had wanted a night club too; she'd taken it for granted. He had suggested the Green Baytree and had been surprised at her prompt refusal. Dick Asher, too, had declined rather quickly. Henry Leggatt had been astonished, for the Green Baytree was fashionable. But he had believed that he understood. In the world of Patricia Leggatt a night club had only to become fashionable to cease to be chic. Too many people went there.

They had gone instead to the Woolly Bear, all three of them. Henry hadn't been delighted that she had asked Dick Asher to join them. She had hailed him in the foyer of the theatre as they were leaving it. He had seemed to be alone, and Dick Asher hadn't the reputation of going about alone. But Henry had done what seemed to be expected, inviting him to join them.

He hadn't been pleased but he had struggled to be reasonable. He knew he danced vilely, and Asher was near-professional. He was very good company too—he was able to be, Henry thought grimly, for he didn't work for a living. He had time to amuse a woman. Leggatt had sighed softly. He mustn't be a stick, a fuddy-duddy spoilsport. He couldn't afford to be.

Just the same there were limits, and it was his unspoken opinion that Patricia had overstepped them. In the Woolly Bear he had nodded, smiling whenever Patricia and Dick Asher returned to their table. He would have allowed that Asher had been very correct. He had asked permission to dance, each time, waking up Leggatt to do so. He had even paid the bill—quietly, unnoticeably. So unnoticeably that Henry, drunk with fatigue and the thrice-used air of a second-class night club, hadn't in fact noticed. By the time they were in the taxi it had been much too late. It would have looked like reluctant afterthought.

So that he couldn't protest when Patricia had been finally inconsiderate. The two of them were in the taxi, Dick Asher at the door. He was smiling still; he'd been smiling all evening. Patricia said suddenly: 'Come back for a drink.'

'I'd like to.'

Henry opened his mouth but shut it again. Dick Asher climbed in quickly.

They drove to Dorset Square, Henry peeping at his watch. It was something between three and four. He was dead on his feet, a little light-headed. After all he'd done a day's work, a hard one as it happened; he'd been working like a horse for months—no, like a conscientious junior Minister. All the hard cases seemed to come to him, whilst Seneschal floated urbanely. Henry Leggatt had begun to wonder about Mr. Seneschal.

God, he was tired. He'd taken his Mecron, naturally, but even Mecron couldn't fuel you for ever. Not at three in the morning and worse. He looked across the cab at Dickie Asher. He was chatting still, smooth and amusing. The evening might just have started.

Henry Leggatt envied him, but he would have admitted he didn't like him. He was handsome as hell if you fancied the debased Greek manner, but Henry didn't much care for Cypriots. He knew it was something to hide and accordingly he hid it. It wasn't politic to risk an accusation of race prejudice, especially when it wasn't true. But there were superior persons who looked at you very oddly if you said anything as honest as that you didn't like Cypriots. Or Indians, or Negroes, or even Gyppos. Perhaps Gyppos was worst of all, since superior people had Gyppos on their conscience. Moreover it was a generalization, and a different sort of superior person gave you a different sort of superior look if you chanced a generalization. Mr. Seneschal, for instance, never ventured one.

But it was no good pretending—not at three in the morning. He simply didn't care much for Cypriots. Dickie Asher in particular.

If that was really his name.

Henry Leggatt paid the taxi at the flat, and the three of them went upstairs. Patricia lit the fire. The flat was centrally heated—Henry thought it too hot already—but Patricia had a feline love of fire. She opened a cupboard, mixing drinks.

Henry slipped away to the bathroom. He washed his hands and face, rocking slightly on his feet. Once or twice he steadied himself against the basin. Above it was a looking glass, and Henry caught his reflection. It frightened him. He looked seventy, he thought, not forty-four. His frank face was ashen, his grey eyes puffed. He looked an old, old man.

Well, he'd been working, working.

He found himself thinking of Mecron, thinking and checking himself. Mecron was for half past six. You took it, lay down a bit, and off you went again. That was what sold it: it unwound you but it set you off again, something the other brands didn't. But Henry didn't want to be set off again; he wanted about ten hours sleep and he didn't look like getting it.

And thinking of Mecron there was that damned great wholesale box of it. The new sales man at Hassertons had sent it him. He wasn't on the board yet, but he meant to be, and it was likely he would get there since he wasn't oversensitive. He'd sent Henry Leggatt a sample box of Mecron. Probably he'd done it innocently, for the directors had had them too. And perfectly properly. The directors could make use of them, slipping a tube to friends and clients, offhandedly recommending. But a Minister couldn't do that, a Minister. . . .

A Minister had been a little apprehensive. He'd put the Mecron in his wardrobe, below his hanging suits. That was the only place for it, since its bulk was considerable. He'd put it there worrying, for Ministers didn't accept presents. That was what it came to. And he could hardly send it back. That would be an insult from an ex-director.

He sat down on the bed, collecting himself. He didn't need Mecron now; he ought to go back to the living-room. After all he was the host. He was also Patricia's husband, and her friendship with Asher worried him. There were a dozen excuses, a dozen self-deceptions, but he knew that if he faced it suspicion would be the word. He ought to go back to them.

He heard his breath escape him, half sigh, half groan. Very slowly he put his legs up.

His wife looked in later and smiled. Then she went back to Asher.

3

COLONEL CHARLES RUSSELL did not know George
Clee very well, but he had met him and he knew his job. He
was senior research chemist at Cameron and Cole, a flyer in
a world which to Russell was as alien as Mars. But though it
was alien he knew that it was important. The senior researcher
at Cameron and Cole was at the top of his profession. He
would have to be, since Cameron and Cole were undeniably
first class, one of perhaps three or four firms, the close-knit
but competitive circle of which Hassertons was also a member. He would be steady as well as brilliant, cautious and hard-
headed, as Cameron and Cole were themselves cautious and
hard-headed. Their aura of Scots reliability was a commercial
asset, at any rate in an England under Social Welfare.

So that when what was almost a stranger had asked for an
urgent interview Russell had agreed at once. He had done so
partly on principle, because in the Security Executive accessi-
bility was a prime rule, and partly from a genuine curiosity.
After all, he told himself, he had recently been reading a report
on drugs, and Cameron and Cole were in just that business.
These things had a habit of linking. Russell had been interested, and he had asked Rachel Borrodaile to attend the
interview. Drugs weren't formally the business of the Executive, but if they should become so the matter would fall in
Miss Borrodaile's bailiwick.

She was a woman of thirty-six but didn't look it. Her
mother had been a Frenchwoman and she was still bilingual.
When the war had ended she had been twenty—twenty and
almost dead. They had found her in a Gestapo cellar, and she
hadn't known her name. For Rachel Borrodaile had been in
the Resistance. Not the sort of Resistance which now lived
in Chelsea or in one of the fashionable arrondissements, nor

the other which talked about its exploits after a drink or two, writing letters to the newspapers about the new betrayal of France, but the genuine working Resistance. She had needed two years in hospital, but finally she had lived. For some reason unknown they hadn't disfigured her: she still had the beautiful skin of the countrywoman, which emphatically she was not. On the contrary Rachel Borrodaile was the essential metropolitan. She dressed mostly in black—elegant, expensive black. She was tall without seeming to be, with the smooth fair hair of a woman ten years younger, and surprisingly gentle eyes. Her shoes she had made for her, but not because she thought it smart. Her right foot wasn't her own, and she had lost it in circumstances which she would never discuss. She walked almost normally but with a faintly authoritative click. Rachel Borrodaile could be authoritative but only when it was necessary. She had the reputation of wealth, and it was known that she had killed two men—strangled them, they told you. Only one had been a German, but both had been interested in looted gold, and gold wasn't difficult to stash away till afterwards. That was the amiable rumour—amiable because Rachel Borrodaile invited amiability. The French had thought her worth That Thing. With Palms, she would explain when pressed, and Diamonds. But she had to be pressed very hard. She was clever and reliable and kind, and a very tough egg indeed. She had never married, and Russell had wondered why.

They were sitting together as George Clee was shown in. Russell hid amusement as he watched his face change slightly into the expression of a man calling on a senior security officer and finding a woman with him, one evidently not a secretary. It was something he had seen before. He introduced Rachel Borrodaile and Clee sat down. Clee said carefully, feeling his way: 'I dare say you're surprised to see me.'

'I'm paid to be surprised. And when I am to hide it.'

George Clee hid a smile in turn. He had been making some discreet inquiries about Colonel Charles Russell, and Russell was living up to the picture which had resulted.

20

'Then would it surprise you if I talked about something called Mecron?'

Russell said blandly: 'I've heard of it.'

'And you know we don't make it ourselves?'

'I do. And I also know who does.'

'You're letting me down very easily. You're saving a great deal of blah.'

'I'll try and save some more. We're heard rumours about Mecron. Stories. Rather disturbing stories.'

'I've come with another.'

'Yes?'

George Clee said slowly: 'One of my young men has just killed a monkey with Mecron. More precisely he drove her mad with it.'

There was a considerable silence which Russell broke. 'Awkward,' he said. 'For you especially.'

'Very awkward indeed. This young man of mine hadn't any business to be playing with Mecron. Dog doesn't eat dog, or not in pharmaceuticals. Moreover a monkey isn't a human being. It's'—Clee hesitated, choosing a word—'it's illustrative,' he said at length, 'evidence of a sort.'

'There seems to be other evidence as well. A gentle fluttering of doctors' wings.'

'I know.'

Russell looked at Rachel Borrodaile. She thought, then nodded briefly. Russell returned to Clee.

'I think you did right to come here.'

'I'm more than relieved. I was afraid you'd send me on to —well, to the orthodox authorities. And what could *they* do? There's no poison in Mecron, and nothing known to be habit-forming. We should be saying that a collection of harmless chemicals, plus one biochemical which nobody admittedly knows much about, was a dangerous and habit-forming drug. Speaking as a chemist I know no reason why that shouldn't happen, but it doesn't often. Prima facie there's a case, but it would take a considerable time to prove it. A habit, by definition, takes time to form. You therefore need time to establish that it exists.'

Russell nodded approvingly. 'Very succinct indeed.'

'Thank you. Moreover, what would the proper authorities do?' Clee put on 'proper authorities' a faint but precise contempt.

Which Russell caught. 'They'd do just what you think they would. They'd flap. It would be just the sort of thing they'd hate. For here's an eminently respectable firm, Hassertons, putting out a drug which is suspect of being a dangerous habit-former. Suspect, but no more, for I gather that it doesn't affect everybody in the same way. Some people seem to be able to take it safely, or at any rate have so far. It's been on the market six months or more, so we'd be conceding that if it *is* habit-forming some people may need more than six months to acquire the habit. That isn't the sort of case an official is likely to jump at.' Russell cocked an eyebrow. 'But is it any sort of sense to a chemist?'

'A chemist couldn't rule it out.'

'Or Mecron might be dangerous to some people, perfectly harmless to others. Is that possible too?'

'Possible. But most unlikely.'

'Then I agree that it's hardly a matter for the orthodox authorities. The Security Executive isn't encouraged to go shooting in other people's woods—I make a point myself of keeping out of them—but I'm not professionally averse from saving a colleague embarrassment. Let's put it like that. For that's what this thing would be—embarrassment. 'There's nothing a civil servant dislikes more than a problem without a rule to cover it. He thinks in terms of authority to do things —laws and the Orders-in-Council so generously made under them. Powers, in fact.' Russell looked directly at George Clee. 'I'm not an expert on the laws which govern drugs, but am I right in guessing that there mightn't be powers in a case like this?'

'I'm not an expert either and I can't be sure. There's a case of a kind.'

'Still pretty thin. Still far from proven.'

'There might be something to cover it, though. Some— some authority.'

'But which somebody would have to invoke. Some civil servant or some politician.'

George Clee looked up quickly, staring in turn at Russell. 'And now I think we're coming to the point.'

'We've come. And I'll make it easy again. Have you heard of Henry Leggatt?'

'Of course. I was thinking about him.'

'He was a director of Hassertons. Now he's a politician.'

'He's Parliamentary Secretary in the Ministry of Welfare.'

Russell had tilted his chair, speaking to the ceiling. 'A drug—very possibly dangerous but far from certain—a drug made by Hassertons, one of whose ex-directors is now a Minister. And maybe there are rules to cover it, maybe there aren't. Perhaps there are powers. But powers must be invoked, applied. Applied by some Minister or at least in his name. And a Minister's a part of government, even a very lowly one. There'd be a scandal perhaps, a rumpus in parliament almost for certain. So the one thing they'd want to avoid would be to put the official clutch in.'

Russell sank into silence and Clee had to prompt him.

'I'd thought that too.'

'Then what do you want me to do?'

'I haven't an idea.'

'I didn't mean the details, but what would you think ideal? We almost certainly can't do it, but it would be something to shoot at.'

George Clee thought it over seriously; at last he said: 'Ideally I'd like an inquiry, a very discreet inquiry in a neutral laboratory. In the circumstances it can hardly go to an official one. The trouble is that it may take some time. Meanwhile I'd like to see this Mecron stopped.'

'Stopped?' Russell had sat up suddenly.

'No further distribution.'

'A tallish order, that.'

'You asked for the ideal.' Clee rose, sketching a gesture of half apology. 'I can see I've set you a problem.'

'We're here at least to listen to them. We'll do what we

23

can and I'll keep in touch with you. In any case, thank you for coming.'

Russell shook hands at the door, coming back to his chair, smiling at Rachel Borrodaile. She knew better than to question him. Instead she said easily: 'An interesting morning.'

'A pretty story, yes. I'd like you to smell around it.' Russell waved a hand. 'You've *carte blanche*, of course. As always.'

'Before I start there's something I ought to tell you. What's called elsewhere a personal interest.'

'But perfectly correct. Exemplary.'

'It's simply that I know Henry Leggatt. Or rather I did.'

'I've never met him myself, though I know his boss. That's Robert Seneschal. I can't say I admire him, but he's a very smooth operator. But tell me about Leggatt.'

'I knew him in the war. He was in one of the Funnies, the things with initials. Most of them were remarkably bogus, but he wasn't in one of those. He wasn't a polo player or an officer in the Brigade who couldn't make it. He was—' for a moment she hesitated—'he was a gallant man.'

'What's he like now?'

'I haven't seen him since, but I shouldn't think he's changed much. He wasn't the type to. He was a square-ish sort of man. I don't mean that as slang, but physically. About five feet nine and much the same shape all round. He wasn't fat but he carried a good deal of muscle. I should think he'd have taken care of himself.'

'Was he clever?'

'Oh no. A certain sort of clever person would have thought him rather stupid. But he wasn't that either. A little slow perhaps, but utterly reliable. Nice reliable face.'

'And you haven't seen him since?'

'I was in hospital for two years, remember.' Rachel Borrodaile rose, putting her weight on her left leg, but rising in one movement, gracefully. 'Besides,' she said, 'he married. Perhaps. . . . Oh, nothing.'

Russell didn't pursue it; he opened the door for her. 'It was proper to tell me but I don't think it matters. Let me know what develops.'

24

He returned to his desk smiling amiably. Russell was most formidable when he was smiling amiably. He looked up a number in an orange directory, picking the red telephone from several. It was his intention to ask Mr. Seneschal to lunch, and at what Russell called his other club. It was one for distinguished layabouts and for bores even more distinguished, and Mr. Seneschal lunched there daily. He always ate the same: potted shrimps, cold beef and salad, though not with pickles since his digestion was suspect, and a half pint of beer drunk slowly. Charles Russell proposed to do better than that, but not very much and for a very good reason. The food at the Mandarins was terrible.

Presently Robert Seneschal was on the line and Russell invited him to luncheon. He said nothing about urgency, but Mr. Seneschal at once accepted. Russell wasn't astonished. He was a modest man, but the head of the Security Executive didn't often ask Ministers to lunch. But when he did the wise ones accepted quickly.

Mr. Robert Seneschal was walking back from his lunch at the Mandarins, across Horse Guards Parade, then down to his ministry. On his left Kent's splendid building shone in the winter sun, but Seneschal frowned at it. It was handsome, he conceded, but it wasn't to his taste; he wouldn't allow it. Mr. Seneschal was a high Anglo-Catholic, and the baroque didn't stir him. He thought it vaguely un-Christian. He was intelligent and had sometimes suspected that these attitudes cost him the price of pleasures too arbitrarily foregone, but he wasn't a man who attached much importance to pleasure.

Nevertheless he was feeling at this moment something very close to it. He was grateful to Charles Russell, but after all it was Russell's business to provide information. What would come afterwards, what action would be taken, was something for subtler minds. His own, for instance. It wasn't unworthy to be feeling confidence, faith in his own ability.

For Robert Seneschal hadn't a doubt that he could handle the matter. It was a three No Trump hand of the sort where he could, if pushed, make four. Three would give him game, though. Naturally Hassertons wouldn't like it—no manufacturer would like stopping distribution of a product which was selling splendidly. But he supposed they had ultimate faith in it; they could hardly refuse a discreet and unofficial check. Not in the circumstances. Seneschal's thin mouth hardened. No, indeed they could not, for they were sensible business men. Robert Seneschal needn't threaten; he needn't even hint at a public inquiry since that, on the known evidence, was bluff, and Hassertons might call it. He had a much better weapon, one much more gothic. For Hassertons made other things than Mecron, and anything up to a third of them was paid for by the Health Service. And Hassertons would realize what that meant. There couldn't be anything crude, of course—no sudden embargo on the house of Hassertons—but Hassertons would know how the machine worked. The orders would tail away, slowly at first and always for some good reason, then faster, faster still. Hassertons would realize that, and Hassertons wouldn't risk it. Seneschal smiled acidly. He had in his hand what he thought of as a sanction, but sanctions apart it was a quid pro quo, almost an arrangement between gentlemen. Hassertons would hold up Mecron for perhaps six months whilst Robert Seneschal arranged for a private check on it. They could hardly object to that even if they wanted to.

Or could, he thought again.

Yes, he'd arrange for a check on Mecron, an independent inquiry. He knew just the man to do it—Hugh Latta of the Templeton laboratory. Dr. Hugh Latta was a member of the Mandarins. Meanwhile he'd contact Hassertons, and that was simple—obvious. It was fortunate that Leggatt had once been with them. He'd scare Leggatt stiff, and Leggatt would scare Hassertons. Good Lord, it was almost easy.

Back in his office he sent for Henry Leggatt. He talked for twenty minutes, smoothly, convincing, enjoying his own skill. Leggatt, he could see, was shaken. He shook him a little more. With apparent reluctance, hesitating on them skilfully, he summoned the final words: career and scandal.

Then he showed Leggatt out. He was thinking, almost gaily, that the man wasn't quite a fool: at least he could accept the obvious. Robert Seneschal put an arm round his shoulders. He did it briefly but with expertise, for it was something he had practised. It didn't pay to acquire the reputation of a cold intellectual. So Robert Seneschal put an arm round his colleagues' shoulders. He also used Christian names a lot, and sometimes he got them right.

Henry Leggatt walked down the corridor to his own room. He told his secretary to make him an urgent appointment with the chairman of Hassertons. She'd find him at the factory. He was chairman but he'd see an ex-director without fuss.

The fuss, Henry thought, came later.

There hadn't been much of it. Russell was saying on a note of irony: 'Seneschal has been good enough to telephone.' He passed Rachel Borrodaile a single sheet of foolscap. 'What do you make of that?'

She read it carefully. 'It looks all right. Hassertons will distribute no more Mecron till the tests are completed, and Seneschal is arranging those. As it happens there's precious little Mecron in the chemists' shops, because a fresh delivery was due next week. Now there won't be one.'

'And how will Hassertons explain it?'

'I imagine they'll talk about a breakdown—technical difficulties. Or the pressure of export orders.' Rachel Borrodaile shrugged. 'The usual nonsense in the trade. I gather they're not short of it.'

'Hm. . . . For how long?'

'Hassertons seem to have fought back a bit and Seneschal agreed. A man called Latta is doing the tests, and they've given him just three months.'

'So that at the end of three months Mecron is either a dangerous drug or it is not. If it isn't, then none of us need worry, and if it's established that it is, our friends—our orthodox friends, the people who are paid for it—can have it dealt with. Quietly, no doubt, since Leggatt would still be involved, but perfectly firmly. Is that how you see it?'

'Yes.'

Russell pulled his beautiful moustache. 'I agree that it looks all right.'

'Yes,' she repeated. 'Yes.'

He looked at her sharply. 'You don't sound too certain.'

'I'm not too certain and I can't say why.' She smiled, excusing herself. 'Call it a woman's hunch.'

'Not something I often bet against.' Russell was decided. 'I wish I felt happier.'

'And so do I. Please let me know when you feel happier.'

CHAPTER

4

THE LITTLE HOUSE in Albert Street was Victorian but by no means graceless. Part of a mid-century development, the developers hadn't been conscienceless. Downstairs a well-kept shop sold the delicacies craved by the Attic palate even in London—*halva, foul medames,* anari cheese, *dolmades* rolled in vine leaves, tinned. For no reason immediately obvious it also sold Irish newspapers. The shop was alive with a vivid babel, the accents of Greece, of County Mayo, the courteous soft sing-song of the Caribbean. Two Cypriot girls served cheerfully. In Camden Town's good living they were running a little to fat, but they were splendid women still. They served as though they enjoyed it, which certainly they did. They had customers, friends, a steady job. They were happy and so was the shop.

Dick Asher had chosen it carefully. Camden Town was a different world from Pont Street but also it was a bridge. That was something he needed. In Camden Town he wouldn't attract attention for he could speak its first language. Nor would his friends, his other friends, meet him there. They might have heard of Camden Town but they'd think of it as a slum. Dick Asher despised them but he took their money; he took, when he could, their women too. Why not? Money and women were serious matters, and serious men were careful of both. When they were not. . . .

When they were not an Asher could live well. Nothing of conscience troubled him. His other world was rotten, decadent. A civilized man was entitled to exploit it.

He went into the little shop, nodding at the women, making a joke which, four miles away, he wouldn't have ventured. One of them threw it back again, and Asher grinned. Four miles away and the comment would have been an insult, but here they all laughed. Asher waved at the girl, conceding best, pushing open the door at the back of the shop. He still had his hat on.

He climbed the stairs and opened another door. The room was surprisingly well furnished, with an air something between an office and a well-used club. There was a sofa, an orderly desk, two telephones, filing cabinets and leather armchairs. In one of them a coal black tom slept comfortably. Of the three men present one was standing. He had killed more than once, but he wouldn't have dreamt of disturbing the tom.

Dick Asher took his hat off, half-sitting on the desk. As the owner he had a right to. The standing man nodded at the table. On it was a wholesale box of Mecron. 'The gen you had was right,' he said. He was speaking a Greek which not every Greek would have easily understood. 'All the directors had a publicity carton of Mecron, and the ex-director Leggatt. I don't know where you get your dope but it's certainly very good.'

'I know Henry Leggatt. Not that he talks to me, but he talks to his wife. Husbands do that innocently and sometimes the wives aren't innocent.'

'I see. I see indeed.'

For an instant Asher was irritated. 'You're not to think my friends are *friends*. You're not to think I live in that world because I like it. I live in it to hear things and I do. It's business—my side of the business.'

'All right, I was only asking.'

Asher nodded at the carton. 'So which one is that?'

'The chairman's. We watched all four as you told us, but the other three had sent the stuff back to the factory.' The standing man's eyebrows rose; he said with a hint of irony: 'Maybe you know why. Maybe you know that too.'

'I think I do. We'll come to that one later.'

'Anyway, this is the chairman's. Probably he was returning it too. He'd parked his car in St. James's Square and we opened the boot with a duplicate. It was as easy as that. . . . Which leaves a box with Leggatt still.'

30

Dick Asher shook his head. 'Too dangerous,' he said. 'I'll handle that one. That is, if we have to.'

'Two gross won't last us long.'

'It shouldn't have to. I've been on to Rikky, of course. By telephone. He'll start on it at once.'

'How long will he need?'

'A fortnight with luck. It should be coming through in a fortnight. Plenty.'

'And then?'

'Then we're away.'

The standing man nodded in turn at the table. 'That carton's pretty hot," he said.

'Perhaps, perhaps not. Which brings me to the other thing. There's a scare about Mecron and a potential political scandal, but for the moment they've smothered it. What they've fixed up is one of those beautifully English official-unofficial inquiries. It's being done by the Templeton laboratory. It's going to take a month or two and until it's finished Hassertons will distribute no more Mecron.' Dick Asher grinned. 'Now if you were Hassertons' chairman . . . ?'

A man in an armchair said thoughtfully: 'I think I see.'

'I'm pretty sure I do. If you were Sir Herbert Hasserton, the fourth generation, you wouldn't much fancy losing a carton of Mecron. Not in the circumstances, the very embarrassing circumstances. You might drive to the nearest police station or again you might not. Remember there's an agreement to put out no more Mecron; you've told your other directors to bring their's back. And what you do yourself is to have your own box stolen. You don't look very bright at best; you may even be suspect of some petty double cross. Remember again you're Sir Herbert Hasserton. And there isn't a trace of the theft you're alleging—no forcing the boot of the car, no evidence that you haven't simply given the stuff away. Or, worse still, sold it. In petty, stupid breach of the agreement. . . . A pretty awkward story, isn't it? Very awkwardly timed. For Sir Herbert Hasserton.'

Somebody laughed appreciatively. 'You think,' he said. 'You can certainly think. Is that all for now?'

'Not quite. The Templeton inquiry is being done by a man called Latta. I want that watched.'

'Why?'

Dick Asher told him.

'This Latta then—you think he'll cook the thing? He'll find Mecron harmless?'

'I think he might.'

'But why again?'

The man in the chair said quietly: 'Lolly, lovely lolly.'

'No,' Asher said, 'it wouldn't be money. Keep an eye on it just the same, though.'

Colonel Charles Russell was dining with Rachel Borrodaile, and, since it was Saturday evening, he had taken her to his club. Not to the Mandarins, for he wouldn't have affronted a woman who knew France as well as she did by offering her food at the Mandarins, and in any case they wouldn't admit women even at week-ends. To the Mandarins women were disturbing and dangerous animals. Instead he had taken her to what he thought of as his proper club. The food was simple but impeccable: salmon, when they had it, came from Scotland not Alaska; the game pie was superb. In the dining-room there was a pleasant smell of Stilton, pervasive but not overpowering. It was all very English, but English cooking at its rare but unmatched best. And the claret was quite first class.

It was a business engagement, for Rachel had said that she wanted to talk to him, but it was also one which Russell had looked forward to. He liked Rachel Borrodaile besides approving her professionally, and she was a distinguished and elegant woman. He wouldn't lose face by taking her to dinner at his club. Quite to the contrary. It wasn't the sort of club where a member would comment on another's woman guest, but Russell knew that Rachel wouldn't pass unnoticed. Nobody passed unnoticed at Bratt's—no woman guest or indeed any other. Rachel would put his stock up. His contemporaries wouldn't comment but they would enviously observe; they'd

32

quietly decide that Charles Russell had excellent taste. There was life in the old dog yet, and an evident discernment.

They were sitting in the drawing-room over coffee and an admirable brandy. Rachel had known better than to bring up business at table, but now she said simply: 'I'm worried about Mecron.'

'I remember I asked you to smell around it.'

'One of your earthier idioms. But I've been doing it.'

'And you don't like what you smell?'

She shook her head but not too hard. Her hair had cost her money.

'Why not?'

'Because I don't understand what's happening. There's Mecron to be had still.'

'To be bought still?' Russell was surprised. 'In the shops? The chemists, you mean? I thought Hassertons had agreed—'

'No, not in the shops. There was a delivery due this week, and now there hasn't been one. That was part of the arrangement which Seneschal made with Hassertons, and Hassertons have kept it. The shops, by and large, are out of Mecron.'

'Nothing has come from the factory?'

'I'm sure of it.'

'If I may ask it—how?'

'We've planted a man there.'

'You have?' Russell said. 'Already?' He looked at Rachel Borrodaile respectfully. 'You don't miss many tricks.' He was thinking that that was true: Rachel Borrodaile didn't miss many tricks. He considered before he asked her: 'So there's Mecron in the market still. Where does it come from?'

'That's what I wish I knew.'

'Who's buying it, then?'

'Addicts,' she said. 'Junkies.'

But he protested at once. 'But you're jumping the gun. We don't know that Mecron is habit-forming. That's what the arrangement was about—Dr. Latta and all of it. We're waiting to find out.'

'The fact remains that you can buy it still.' Rachel Borrodaile drank some brandy. 'That is, if you want it badly enough, and provided you're willing to pay for it. The price in the chemists was nine-and-six a tube of twenty, for it was never cheap. And now you can buy it on the black—three pounds a tube if you're lucky.'

'That's being paid for it?'

'And more.'

'By whom?'

'By addicts,' she repeated.

Russell ordered fresh coffee and brandy with it. Rachel poured the coffee from the magnificent silver pot, and Russell thought intently. Finally he asked her: 'What sort of people are they?'

'From our point of view the worst. They're perfectly respectable people—executives.' Her grimace defined executives. 'I talked about junkies, but these aren't junkies in an ordinary context. You remember that report I sent you? The drug addict is normally either very rich or very poor, but these aren't either. They're hardworking men, and women too—almost certainly too hardworking. They've found Mecron helps them. It helps them so much they'll go into the black for it. It's not yet a crime, there's no law against Mecron, and in any case they could always say that they had bought it quite openly a week ago. The whole thing breaks '—she hesitated—'breaks the accepted rules.'

'Which you're as attached to as I am. You don't like to see a pattern broken.' Russell thought again. 'You spoke of the black market—what black market?'

'I haven't found out all of it, but you can buy it in a Turkish Bath. You can get it from the hall porters of two expensive but not quite first-class hotels. You can buy it in at least one restaurant.'

'What sort of restaurant?' Russell had asked it idly.

'A Cypriot restaurant.'

He sat up suddenly but didn't have to ask her. She went on quietly.

'I know what you're thinking. Narcotics—authentically prescribed narcotics—aren't a problem in England, or not on the American scale. They're peddled, of course, but that's

34

about the word for it. Our colleagues aren't up against wide-spread well-organized rings with all the trimmings of political protection. If we've a drug problem the Americans envy us, and most of the Continentals. To them it looks small time. But in so far as it exists the Cypriots are in it. They're in most things with money attached. Women, for instance. There's an—an organization in being.'

'I've heard of it. I agree it's not a major problem, but then you're not saying it is. Or not at the moment. You're saying it has *potential*, saying—'

'I'm saying that if Mecron really spread, really grew serious, there'd be a brand new market of a quite new kind. Something on a quite new scale.'

'If it really does form habit.'

She said softly: 'I've noticed you haven't denied it.'

Another couple had come into the drawing-room. Russell was charitable, and he was prepared to give the man the benefit of the doubt; he was prepared to assume that the younger and very dowdy woman was his niece. He didn't know her but he knew all about Sir Jonathan. He was an ex-consul general whom a convenient war had promoted to a rank and honour which he could hardly have anticipated. And he was notoriously ga-ga; he wrote facetious comments on the secretary's notices; and he had very long ears indeed.

Russell said: 'Excuse me a moment,' slipping away to the library. He consulted a book of reference, returning with a waiter and another tray. 'Since we're going to speak French I thought that a little champagne . . . I know we've drunk brandy, I dare say I'm a criminal, but this one won't hurt you. At any time or after anything.' For the first time Russell was really serious, for wine was a serious matter. 'I promise you.'

Rachel Borrodaile didn't comment. It was one of the things he admired in her: she never asked unnecessary questions. They began to talk again in fluent idiomatic French, Russell with perfect confidence, since the reference book had reassured him. It had told him that Sir Jonathan had served in France—five years on and off—and Sir Jonathan had been a diplomat. That is if a consul counted. He'd been a diplomat in France. Russell was certain he wouldn't understand colloquial French.

They had disposed of the bottle before Rachel returned to business. She stretched her long legs reflectively, considering her beautiful shoes; she said in near-argot: 'There's something else. It isn't really relevant—'

'Everything's relevant.'

'So you've always taught me. But this one could be nothing, even to the Executive.'

'Tell me,' he said.

'You remember George Clee's young man—the one who killed the monkey?'

'I never heard his name.'

'I have. It's Ronald Davis.'

'It rings no bell with me.'

'It isn't supposed to. But Ron Davis has a brother.'

'Yes?'

'A brother called Peter Davis.'

Russell shook his head. 'No click again.'

'This Peter Davis is a civil servant. He's an Assistant Principal, and he's working as Henry Leggatt's secretary.'

Charles Russell thought it over. 'Coincidence,' he said at length, 'is always extremely untidy.'

'And when it's not significant, when you don't see which way it's breaking—'

'I find it most alarming.' Russell reflected again. 'Is anything known about either of them?'

'Nothing that matters. There's a file on Peter Davis, but it's the ordinary file on everyone with heavy left-wing views. The progressive beards—all those.' Rachel laughed. 'We call them the advanced class.'

'There's nothing on this file?'

'Nothing but foolishness.'

'Fools,' Russell said, 'are hell.'

5

LATE ON MONDAY evening Rachel Borrodaile was sitting
in the Security Executive reading the considerable mass of
paper on the Davis brothers which the machine had thrown
up to her. She wasn't surprised at its extent, since an inquiry
by a senior official of the Executive about almost any individual in the country would produce within hours a formidable dossier.

She began on Ronald Davis, smiling approval. He seemed
a delightful young man. He had a job he liked and a lively
curiosity into its byeways; he had an adequate salary and a
wide range of interests on which to spend it; he was fond of
travel and his habits were wholly orthodox. He was an extrovert, she decided, whatever the pundits had currently determined a useful word meant. She knew one when she saw him,
and it was a type she liked. Come to think of it, if he had
been fifteen years older she might have been personally interested in Ronald Davis.

For a moment she let her mind wander. . . . After all she
was thirty-six. She had a clear picture of Rachel Borrodaile,
one she could tell herself was innocent of the stupider illu-
sions, but nobody could be sure that their image of themselves
was the image that others saw. . . . A competent, highly
efficient officer? She has solid reason to suppose that they
saw that. But the typical bachelor girl, a bit of a battle-axe or
slipping within distance of it? That wasn't such a pleasant
thought. She was a woman still.

She looked again at the papers before her, unsmiling now,
for she saw nothing amusing in Peter Davis. He could hardly
be more different from his brother. Rachel was sorry for him
—goodness, how earnest he was, gracious, how he must worry.
And often with good reason. A great deal was wrong with a

lunatic world, plenty was wrong on your own front doorstep: the fools in high places, greed and, right or left, a differing but always vast complacency. You couldn't contract out, not even if you had dared to try. But not all the time, she thought —not all of it. One mustn't become a bore, and Peter Davis sounded one.

She collected her thoughts sharply. All this was the aura of Peter Davis, the background of a certain sort of clever young man, but it wasn't the facts. She returned to them with professional attention. The facts were that Peter Davis had extremely left-wing views. His contacts had been worth checking but, though significant, none had been positive. Rachel sighed softly. The Executive had several thousand files on people like Peter Davis, and in ninety-nine cases in a hundred nothing came out of them. And they had one thing in common, the inability to act effectively. Finally they snuffed out.

But one in a hundred wasn't quite ineffective, one in a hundred acted. Rachel's business at bottom was to guess whether Peter Davis was that one, to guess and to tell Charles Russell. She shook her head slowly, putting the new reports on to the existing file. Peter Davis hadn't the smell of action, and moreover a security officer must ask herself what action. Peter Davis was brother to the man who had been conducting a highly irregular experiment with Mecron, and he was also private secretary to a Minister who had once been connected with the firm which made it. It was a coincidence, meat and drink to the Executive, but what could this Davis do? Assuming, that is, that his brother had told him that Mecron might be dangerous. That had to be assumed. In which case Peter Davis would know about a potentially dangerous drug, something anti-social—that would be his word for it—something not yet controlled, though obviously it ought to be, something which his Minister's firm was doing very well from.

Peter Davis would smell drains at once—privilege, wicked profits, graft in high places. . . .

Rachel Borrodaile frowned, for she hadn't much faith in her ability to think like Peter Davis. It was a habit of mind, a political reflex, and it wasn't her own. In any case what could

38

he *do*? Finally he was a civil servant, and there was no safer niche for a left-wing woolly than a job in the civil service.

Ron Davis was moving to the record-player, exchanging a disc by Fats Waller for another by Fats Waller. He was interested in jazz but aware that he had friends in that world who considered his tastes antiquated and himself a terrible old square. It did not trouble him, since he seldom worried about other people's opinions. Meanwhile he enjoyed Mr. Waller.

His brother said irritably from his chair: 'For heaven's sake.'

'What's eating you? You know the arrangement—half an hour for you and half an hour for me. I've five minutes to go still. Then you can have what you like. What *would* you like?'

'I was thinking of some opera.'

'Good. Then I may have it both ways. I like opera too, though it has to be the right sort of opera. I can't stand the prissified kind. I like good red meat and lots of gravy. I like melodramatic sopranos bursting their stays. I like tenors who do everything they shouldn't. I like the San Carlo, and I adore it when they whip the slaves down the steps in the arena at Verona. Ponchielli *isn't* a dirty word. I don't like having to put on evening dress in the middle of the afternoon—I hate it at any time. I like touring companies in little towns in Italy you've never heard of. I like ham and more ham, I—'

'Oh God, oh God, oh God!'

For a moment Mr. Waller's superlative left hand relaxed, and in the comparative quiet Ronald Davis looked at his brother. He knew him very well, and it was evident that the exclamation hadn't been one of aesthetic disapproval. Peter Davis wasn't being hoity-toity; Peter Davis was in travail. Ronald switched off the record-player. He turned up the gas fire and moved to a chair by Peter's. They sat for a moment in silence, then Ronald asked simply: 'Well?'

'Oh, it's nothing.'

'I can see that it's nothing. Like hell. I think you'd better tell me.'

'You remember that monkey?' Peter's tone was a mixture of reluctance and relief.

'Monkey? Ermyntrude, you mean? I'd got quite fond of her.'

'But you killed her.'

'I had to.'

'I didn't mean at the end. But you told me you filled her up with Mecron. Why did you do that?'

Ron Davis rubbed his chin. 'For no reason I could really justify as a scientist, certainly not as a scientist employed by Cameron and Cole, not Hassertons. The fact is I'd been using the stuff. Then one evening I thought of it, and I knew I was wanting it bad. So I didn't take it—I'm a chemist, remember. Then I heard one or two stories, doctors and so on, and I began to get curious. I got curious enough to try Mecron on a monkey.'

'Proving it's a habit-forming drug.'

Ron Davis sat up sharply. 'Stuff and nonsense.' He was genuinely indignant. 'You may be very good at economics—all that L.S.E. stuff—but you don't know a thing about science, far less about proper proof. What I've established is that Mecron in massive doses wasn't good for a monkey. Monkeys aren't human beings, a single monkey in particular. In any case I grossly over-dosed her.'

'But the craving you felt yourself. And all those doctors' stories.'

Ron Davis considered again before he said deliberately: 'If you want it in lawyers' language there's a prima facie case.'

'Well, there you are.'

'Oh, do try and think sensibly. A case—oh yes—but a prima facie case that Mecron may not be all it's made out to be. It may—repeat may—have secondary effects that nobody has so far spotted.'

'It's a shameful capitalist racket. The stuff's a poison.'

'Say that outside and see what happens.'

'But you admitted there was a case.'

'Simply something to start from. Mecron may need looking at.'

'Then what are you going to do about it?'

'Me?' Ronald Davis was unaffectedly astonished. 'Me? Stick my neck out?'

'But you've a duty to the public.'

Ron Davis said something about the public. 'In any event something *is* being done. The gup in the business is that Hassertons have agreed to put out no more Mecron whilst somebody has a proper look at it. That will involve controls, if an economist knows what that means—everything I didn't do myself in my own half-baked experiment. That wouldn't stand up for a minute. Instead they'll make a job of it.'

'Who's going to do it?'

'A man called Latta. Dr. Hugh Latta of the Templeton laboratory.'

'What sort of a man is Latta?'

'Frankly, he wouldn't have been my own choice. The Templeton is first class still, but Latta'—Ron Davis shrugged —'Latta's a bit of a has-been. By now he's what I should call a scientific administrator rather than a scientist, but he has splendid people under him. They'll do the work and he'll push the paper in. I shouldn't wonder if they knighted him. He must be overdue for it.'

'How long will it take?'

'They tell me three months. I should have wanted more myself.'

'Three months!' Peter Davis was out of his chair. 'In three months' time a thousand people could be addicts.'

'With nothing more on sale? With no Mecron in the shops?'

'That's why I said a thousand, not a hundred thousand. There'll be Mecron in private hands still. People will have bought it—stocked it up. They'll go on taking it, forming the habit.'

'If it does form habit.'

41

'Can you tell me it doesn't?'

'No.'

'*Then what are you going to do?*'

'Listen.' Ron Davis was very quiet. 'Listen to me carefully. Anybody who attacks Mecron on the evidence available is asking for trouble. And I mean big trouble. Myself in particular. I work for Cameron and Cole and I hadn't any mandate to be monkeying with another firm's product.'

'You should make what you know public. Now.'

'Bah. The public isn't entitled to judge what it wouldn't understand, and if I went to another chemist he'd tell me I was crazy. And perfectly rightly. He'd want a hundred Ermyntrudes, controls, proper dosage, a respectable experiment. He'd tell me to go back to school.'

Ronald was still patient but his brother was rigid. Ronald didn't like the look of him. Peter said tensely: 'But addiction. The risk. The community—'

'You mentioned a thousand people.'

'They're part of the community.'

Ron Davis said slowly, finally: 'I pass. In this sort of thing we haven't a language in common.' He looked at his brother and then at the clock. 'It's only half past ten. The Green Baytree will be waking up. I'll stand you an evening. You look pretty low and I'll cheer you up.'

'The Green Baytree wouldn't cheer me up.'

'Why ever not?' Ron Davis couldn't understand it.

'We haven't a language in common.'

'All right, I'll go alone. I'm not sitting here with a death's-head.' Ron Davis grinned. 'I might see that piece again—your Minister's very approachable-looking wife. Not to mention the dago boy friend.'

'Oh, shut up.'

They didn't often quarrel.

Ron Davis went to the bathroom, shaving again. When he returned to the living-room his brother hadn't moved. Ron looked at him with real compassion. He was fond of Peter, but he thought him a strange old stick, too old for his age but a bit of a baby.

42

'You won't change your mind?'

'You're quite without conscience, quite irresponsible.'

Ron Davis went out but his brother sat on quietly. He'd suddenly seen his duty. It would ruin him, of course: his career in the civil service would be finished. They might not be able to tie it to him, or not as a formal charge which he would have to answer, but naturally they'd be bound to guess. And Establishments had elephantine memories. He'd go as far as Principal and stop there, always in the dimmest posts, a devil for younger men. It would be difficult to find a job outside the service. He wasn't trained for anything but minuting; he couldn't produce and he couldn't sell. He'd be finished indeed.

For a moment he felt a wild release, a martyr's exaltation. Peter Davis would be finished but Peter Davis would be justified. He wouldn't have lived quite uselessly.

He put on his hat and coat and found a taxi, directing it to the offices of *The Gong*. *The Gong*, he knew, would do it; *The Gong* would be delighted to. Though in public it supported the party's policies it held them in private in a measureless contempt. Once it had challenged them head on and been both roundly snubbed and openly defeated. *The Gong* had a very thick skin and the snub hadn't hurt it. But the defeat had been much more serious. *The Gong* didn't fancy defeats, open defeats especially.

And somewhere in *The Gong*'s huge hive Peter Davis would admit to an acquaintance. He wasn't at all a close one, but he was something called a feature man.

He received Peter Davis politely, making no comment but listening carefully. He made a note or two and asked three questions. He thanked Peter Davis and let him go.

He then ran up four flights of stairs wishing that he were fitter. His editor raised his eyebrows but gave him a chair in silence. He was an experienced feature man, and experienced staff didn't come bursting in for nothing. No indeed.

The editor in turn listened without interruption. He asked a question but only one. The answer seemed to be satisfactory. The editor thought, then picked up a telephone. Into it he said three words, and somewhere in the paper's shameless womb a muted rumble hesitated; finally died away.

The editor looked at the feature man with a very strange expression; he said almost shamefacedly: 'I've heard about doing that—as a myth of the trade. But I've never yet done it. In practice I've never dared. It can cost half a million copies.'

'If it hurts you know who—really hurts him—I think you'll keep your job.'

'I could lose it either way. One day I'll work for a newspaper. A proper one.' The editor sighed. 'We all say that but we all like money.' He picked up another telephone. Looking at the feature man he said: 'I'm ringing the Patron.'

In an ugly white house on a beautiful beach the man they called the Patron had just gone to bed. A servant woke him reluctantly, for he was an irascible man. He snapped irascibly: 'Well?'

'It's a call from the office, sir.'

'Can't they run the flaming paper?'

'I was to say it was urgentest, sir.'

'It's always urgentest. Who's calling?'

The servant told him and the Patron seemed appeased. He thought nothing of his directors, but the editor hadn't the reputation of panicking unnecessarily.

'Put him through here to the bed.'

The man *The Gong* called Patron listened intently, his florid face hardening. He didn't consider and he didn't hesitate; instead he said shortly: 'Run it. Front page, of course. Clear it with the lawyers. 'Bye.'

He climbed out of bed, pulling on a dressing-gown, smiling and ringing the bell. This called for a bottle and he sent his servant to bring it. His doctors had forbidden him alcohol, but this was a special case, a celebration.

This was very sweet indeed.

6

HENRY LEGGATT HAD hardly settled at his desk next morning when Peter Davis interrupted him. He was looking very white and Henry noticed it. He was a considerate man and he spoke in sympathy.

'You're not looking well.'

'It's nothing. Perhaps it's a touch of 'flu.'

'Why don't you go home?'

'Thank you, but I can manage.'

'But so could I.'

This Peter Davis ignored; he said a little shakily: 'The Press Officer is here. He said it was urgent.'

'Then have him in at once, please.'

The Press Officer came in noiselessly on the rubber-soled shoes he always wore. He suffered from some complicated foot complaint with a Latin-Greek title medically bastardized. Its existence hadn't escaped his colleagues. He was known as the Creeper or, by the more junior and ribald, simply as Mister Feet. Like all government Press Officers he was quite without weight with journalists, in whose hard world he had conspicuously failed. Finally he had found his niche in the Ministry of Social Welfare, soon parodying the manner of the genuine administrative class. He never answered promptly, but pondered weightily; he ruminated, pursing his lips; finally he begged the question. He was personally disliked and privately despised.

Now he slipped into a chair without being asked to, but not before sliding on to Leggatt's desk the morning edition of *The Gong*. He sat in his chair looking lugubrious. This he did successfully, for he was feeling miserable, but he was also trying to look helpful, on top of the thing, and in this he failed. He hadn't in fact the least idea what to do about *The*

Gong. Nobody had ever the least idea what to do about *The Gong.*

The Press Officer thought it horribly unfair.

Henry Leggatt began to read below the flaring headline. He looked at the Press Officer, but the Press Officer was staring at his deplorable feet. Henry read on quickly.

He decided that it was competent, very professional journalism. *The Gong* wasn't the sort of newspaper to worry about the mere possibility of an action in the courts, but it had very good lawyers, and of the four defences conceivable all had been carefully left open. A suit might succeed or again it might not, but it wouldn't be open-and-shut—no having to settle ignominiously out of court—and in any case the publicity would be more valuable than any likely damages.

The page began quite quietly. Mecron was named but it wasn't openly abused: on the contrary there was a meticulously fair statement of its claims and history. Mecron wasn't a poison, nor known to be dangerous in any way whatsoever. Nevertheless. . . .

Henry couldn't help smiling, for what followed was expertly done. Doctors unnamed ('But I bet they could produce some if they had to') had begun to wonder about certain secondary effects. Experiments had been conducted which. . . .

The next paragraph was masterly. Analysed carefully it said nothing whatever, but three million spines would chill deliciously. Then came the lead-in: naturally there were rules and regulations in a matter of this kind. The authorities weren't without powers if they chose to invoke them.

Why didn't they invoke them?

And finally, after the sparring, came the measured, deliberate blow. It was factual and, if read alone, quite unexceptionable. It was a simple statement that Mecron was manufactured by a firm called Hassertons, of which Mr. Henry Leggatt, M.P., had been a director until quite recently. And it would be recalled that Mr. Leggatt was now Parliamentary Secretary to the Ministry of Social Welfare.

There wasn't a vestige of improper emphasis: the paragraph wasn't indented and the type was normal. The reader could take it or leave it.

Most, very clearly, would take.

Henry read the two columns again, anger and admiration wrestling. He turned at last to the Press Officer.

'Has the Solicitor seen this?'

'He's studying it now. There was some talk of consulting counsel.'

'Curse counsel—there isn't time. Have you spoken to the Solicitor yourself?'

'Just a word, sir.' The Press Officer was being cagey.

'What did he say?'

The Press Officer didn't like it. The ministry's Solicitor was the stuffiest of officials, self-important even by the standards of Departmental lawyers. Which were very high standards of self-importance. The Solicitor wouldn't like to be reported; he'd wish to speak himself. The Press Officer said uncomfortably: 'I think he'd prefer to see you, sir.'

'Of course he would, and so he shall. I'll talk to him when he's had time to think. Meanwhile we've got to act on this, and quick. What were his first reactions?'

'Not very happy, sir.'

'Naturally they weren't.' Henry Leggatt controlled himself, asking with a crisp patience: 'But what did he say?'

'He said you could probably sue—get an action on its legs were his actual words.'

'And was I likely to succeed?'

The Press Officer mopped his forehead with yesterday's handkerchief; he put it away and for a moment thought. Then he held his right hand out, clenched, flipping the thumb upwards, tossing an imaginary coin.

Henry said softly: 'I see.'

They sat for some time in silence till Peter Davis came in again.

'Mr. Seneschal would like to see you, sir.'

'I'll come at once.' Henry Leggatt rose, smiling politely at the Press Officer, though he had quite forgotten him. He

47

was an easy man to forget. Henry walked along the corridor and knocked.

'Come in.'

Robert Seneschal had *The Gong* on his desk, and his handsome donnish face, normally rather pale, was a very undonnish crimson. He waved a long hand at *The Gong* but snapped at Henry Leggatt.

'You've seen this rag?'

'I have.'

'May I ask what you're going to do?'

'I'm going to see my private lawyers, but I've more than an inkling what they'll advise me. They'll say there's a case but by no means a certain one.'

Seneschal said deliberately: 'I should be grateful if you would take no action—private action—without first consulting me.'

'By all means. But why?'

'There's a political side to this besides the personal.'

'Oh, that.' Henry answered unhesitatingly for he had already made his mind up. 'Naturally I'd thought about that. I'll resign if you want me to.'

Robert Seneschal stared at him. Henry couldn't read his expression for he had never before seen it. Irritation was there, and reluctant respect, and something that might almost have been envy. Finally Seneschal said acidly: 'I must beg you to think. How *can* you resign? They'd take it as an immediate admission that something was wrong with Mecron. Tomorrow's *Gong* would splash it again, and from their point of view they'd be perfectly justified. And anything might happen then. Anything.'

'Then what do you want me to do?'

'Not to play into their hands. Sit tight and—and be silent. You must leave this to me.'

'And what will you do?'

Seneschal smiled thinly. It was doubtful whether he intended to be patronizing, but he contrived the impression that he thought Henry Leggatt a little naïve. He said in his lecturer's English: 'We've an answer, you know; we've an

48

arrangement with Hassertons about Mecron. I'll speak to the Home Secretary, and I'll arrange a helpful Question if the Opposition hasn't already tabled a loaded one. In either case there's an answer. For the moment.'

'But myself, my own position—'

'I should deprecate anything rash.'

Henry Leggatt went back to his own room. He had been dismissed and knew it. A Parliamentary Secretary didn't really count: his job didn't matter. Henry had accepted it since he wasn't conceited, but there was something else and it had begun to frighten him. For Henry Leggatt didn't count; he wasn't, to them, a *person*. He was expendable as every junior Minister was expendable, but only when there was advantage in expending him. He wasn't allowed to expend himself, the choice wasn't his. They'd ditch him if it paid them—good God, they wouldn't hesitate—but he mustn't ditch himself. Not when it might embarrass them.

At his desk he sighed uneasily. Meanwhile there was a mess—Patricia and Dick Asher, Mecron and *The Gong*. . . .

Sometime he'd think it out.

Which Russell and Rachel Borrodaile were already doing. Russell was holding *The Gong*. He wasn't wearing gloves but somehow conveyed that he was missing them. He looked at *The Gong* again, then dropped it in the wastebasket, turning to Rachel.

'It's a very neat smear, of course. Where do you think they got it?'

'I don't know that—not yet.'

'Care to guess?'

She shrugged. 'One of the two Davis brothers probably.'

'Quite so. But which?'

'It would hardly have been Ronald—not on what we know of him. On what we know of him I like Ronald Davis.'

'Then it's Peter?'

'Yes, that would fit.'

Russell nodded agreement. 'It would fit all too well. Not

that we need bother about that aspect of it, since Peter Davis's masters are more than capable of dealing with him. I don't suppose he got his information from anything official—nothing across his Minister's desk—so the Official Secrets Act won't be in question. Nevertheless Peter Davis's superiors will deal with him. In their own queer fashion.'

'But if he didn't get his information officially, he must have got it from his brother. They share a flat, you know.'

'Which would be awkward for Ronald. Cameron and Cole wouldn't be pleased with him.' Russell looked up suddenly. 'I can guess what you're thinking.'

'You're uncommonly sharp.'

'You've an uncommon sense of justice. Just as well in a security officer. All right, I'll speak to Clee. We promised to keep in touch with him. I'll mention Ronald Davis though I can't make promises. But I'll try and help him.'

'You're an understanding man.'

'In this place a man who isn't soon becomes a menace. . . . Now where were we?'

'We were looking at a large-ish leak in *The Gong*. It says in effect that something is wrong with Mecron, and it links up Mecron with a junior Minister. Politically it could be dynamite. To Ministers—all of them.'

'Hm. . . . But they've a comeback and a fair one—the stop on Mecron's distribution to the shops and the Latta inquiry. There'll be Question and Answer in the House, probably several. It'll go to the Home Secretary. I could think of an awkward Supplementary or two, but the Home Secretary is normally a very good bat on a turning wicket. Maybe *The Gong* knew about Seneschal's arrangement with Hassertons and maybe it didn't. In either case it wouldn't have stopped them. It's the first attack that counts, and some mud always sticks.' Russell considered. 'But I don't think the political side concerns us yet.'

'Then where do we go from here?'

Russell didn't answer at once, and Rachel walked to the window. She moved with her tiny limp, but gracefully. Russell looked at her long waist with pleasure, her elegant crupper.

She would be wearing something, he supposed, but it wouldn't be anything severe. In any case he didn't hold it against her. All sensible women wore something.

Presently she returned to the chair by Russell's desk. Her question was still unanswered but instead she asked another.

'You remember I told you there was Mecron in circulation still—stuff being handled on the black?'

'Of course I do.'

'And I told you what we then knew about who was handling it. It was a couple of not quite first-class hotels, a Turkish bath, a Cypriot restaurant. And the police have been helpful about those, for to them it's the usual people. I'd call it a gang if I didn't have to watch your face if I used the word. But there they are—small beer by American standards, but an organization in being I think I once stuffily called it, and pretty well organized at that. What ordinary narcotics traffic there is they mostly seem to handle. There are women and blackmail on the side, and they're capable of strong-arm stuff as well. Oh yes, indeed. The police suspect a murder too, but they haven't been able to pin it. They're tied in with another lot in Liverpool, and they've working arrangements with several others. They're not to be taken lightly. And I take no credit for any of this, for the police passed it out on a platter.'

'And this—all right, we'll call it a gang—this gang has its hands on some Mecron? Which they're peddling?'

'Yes. And to quite new people.'

'I know. I realize the implications.' Russell rubbed his chin. 'And another thing occurs to me. This set-up must be pretty sure Mecron *is* habit-forming, and they must be pretty confident it's going to be found so officially. Otherwise the game would hardly be worth the candle. Passing around a small unexplained quantity of a drug which is going to be on open sale again in a few months doesn't sound like your Cypriots at all. They're nothing if not excellent business men. But if it's going to be declared dangerous then it'd be well worth keeping the pot boiling with the odd consignment, especially if they've a new type of client. Habits can be formed but they can also be broken, and broken they often are when the drug

51

in question is literally unobtainable. So the odd parcel of Mecron would attract them strongly. After that, after it's made illegal, Mecron would be a narcotic like the others, something to be made abroad and smuggled in.' Russell made a gesture of disgust. 'Like heroin and all the rest of them, but with a quite new brand of addict, one much more respectable and therefore much easier to put the bite on. For I gather that's the obverse of their business. Blackmail.'

'That's the normal sequence.' Rachel waited, then asked her first question again. 'So where do we go from here?'

'I wish I could tell you, I wish I could do more than analyse. Politically we're not in this, or not for the present if the Home Secretary handles it cleverly. But it's the other side that worries me. Perhaps that's not strictly our business either, but I just don't fancy the idea of a probably corruptive tranquillizer being peddled around. . . . Existing habits strengthened, possibly new addicts formed.' Russell grunted. 'I don't think I've the reputation of a too tender social conscience, but I have one at bottom and I just don't like this thing. It's not officially our business, but I should plead, if I had to, that it's nobody else's. The Dangerous Drugs people can hardly commit themselves very far with a drug which isn't yet known to be dangerous, and it isn't straight police work. So I'll arrogate jurisdiction to the Executive, if only on the principle that we're here to pick the bits up. We've often had to do it. Unhappily the only thing that occurs to me is obvious: find out where this Mecron comes from. That's no solution in itself but it might be a line.'

'We're working on that. We've a man in Hassertons and quite a few others involved.'

'Good.' Russell started to rise but Rachel didn't; she said deliberately: 'Something else has struck me.'

Russell sat down again. When something struck Rachel Borrodaile it was usually worth attention.

'Yes?'

'We've accepted the assumption that the Cypriots are convinced Mecron's dangerous. Are you?'

'Frankly, I strongly suspect it.'

'Then our friends won't be worried by this smear in *The Gong*. What would worry them would be if Mecron were found harmless.'

'Quite.'

'*Then what about Hugh Latta?*'

Charles Russell sat up sharply. 'I know that voice,' he said. 'Explain.'

'We know nothing about him.'

'We know he's an eminent chemist. He's head of the Templeton laboratory.'

'We know nothing about the man.'

'You think that we should?'

She said softly: 'I'd feel happier. A lot depends on him.'

'He's a scientist with a scientist's training. And presumably his disciplines.'

'He's a disappointed man.'

'Then you *do* know something about him.'

Her shoulders rose and fell. 'One hears things,' she said.

'What other things?' Russell hadn't meant to sound abrupt.

'Nothing I could write, so nothing I ought to say.'

'A pricking of the thumbs again?'

'I'm afraid so.'

'Accepted,' Russell said. 'Accepted with thanks.' He didn't speak in irony.

He thought for some time again, then asked: 'George Clee is a chemist too. Do you think he would help? Or could?'

'It's a pretty small world, top chemists'.'

But Russell had made his decision. 'I was to talk to George Clee, you remember, so I'll bring up Ronald Davis, but I'll mention Hugh Latta too. Clee may not talk, of course; he may think I'm a foolish old man.'

'Buy him a good meal,' she said.

'I will.'

Doctor Hugh Latta too had seen *The Gong*. He had noticed it, folded, on a table in his club, but he hadn't picked it up, for at the Mandarins *The Gong* wasn't a good status symbol. You read *The Times*, or better *The Guardian*, or, with the faint air of patronage which the members soon acquired, *The Daily Telegraph*. But not *The Gong*. *The Gong* went on a table in the smoking-room, the headline uppermost. The Mandarins could glance at what the rag was up to, but they mustn't be seen reading it.

Hugh Latta bought a copy going home, reading it in his flat. It made him angry: he thought it an impertinence. He was conducting a scientific inquiry, one commissioned by a Minister, though not yet officially. And *The Gong* had pre-judged it. It was a scandal, a public outrage. Mecron could still be found innocuous.

He moved to his desk. The preliminary reports from the laboratory had begun to come in, and he read them thoughtfully. Naturally they were only preliminary reports and it would have been grossly unscientific to form any opinion on them. There was most of three months left, and Latta would have liked much more. Now with *The Gong* stepping in he wouldn't be surprised if he were asked to cut it. And that wouldn't suit him—not as a scientist.

He read the reports again, very attentively, shrugging. They broke about fifty-fifty, and fifty-fifty might not suit him either.

Not as a man.

7

RACHEL BORRODAILE WAS at her hairdresser's. She needed nothing doing to her hair, and she had called in office time. Neither disturbed her, since Rachel and her hairdresser were in professional relations.

In the Security Executive words like block and guard, agent and even contact were considered a little chi-chi. They belonged to a world which the Executive both understood and used, but they weren't its own idiom. It spoke instead of 'the machine', or sometimes of 'my people'.

Rachel's hairdresser was one of her people.

Now she was doing something unnecessary to Rachel's beautiful hair. When she had finished she picked up her handbag. Rachel wasn't outraged when she coolly opened it. The girl dropped in an envelope, shutting the bag again.

'That will be four pounds ten.'

Rachel paid without comment. Later she would charge it, for four pounds ten was the standard rate for what was called a postman.

In her taxi back to the Executive she read the note. It wasn't from the girl and she hadn't expected it. The girl was a carrier, for it was a principle in the Executive that its agents should know only one person above them and that that person shouldn't be one of the Executive's officials. That couldn't always be managed, and with old hands it was often waived. But the man planted in Hassertons wasn't yet privileged. He reported to an assistant in a fashionable Bond Street hairdresser's.

Rachel in her taxi smiled. It wasn't a bad rule, though amateurs overdid it. In the Resistance, for example, it had saved uncounted lives. But then that hadn't been amateur, or not the part that counted.

She looked at her foot, not smiling now. That hadn't been amateur either; that hadn't been something to smile at.

She read the report again. Its English was over-careful, but as information it was excellent:

So far as I have been able to ascertain Hassertons have kept their side of the bargain. There are considerable stocks of Mecron, because a distribution to the chemists was due to take place two days after the arrangement was reached that nothing further should go out, and in any case there was more than a week's supply in hand. But within the limits of what I have been able to do with discretion I feel confident that none has been leaving the factory. However, I have learned something else. Shortly before the dead-line date the sales director gave a wholesale carton of Mecron to each of the four directors with a view to private publicity. (A wholesale carton contains 288 tubes of 20 tablets each.) He also sent a carton to Mr. Henry Leggatt, a Member of Parliament and an ex-director.
I pass this information for what it may be worth.

Rachel thought it over. This was confirmation and to some extent a limit. Five cartons of Mecron were out, a sort of joker, and the Cypriots had got one of them, for it was a safe rule never to assume more than was necessary, and a single box of Mecron, two gross of it, would account for what was being handled on the black. That meant that one of four directors had been careless or inconveniently openhanded with a wholesale carton of Mecron, since it was inconceivable that Henry Leggatt would have parted with a drug which he knew was suspect. So three cartons remained with three other directors, but those could hardly be a danger. No sensible firm would have left them floating: it would have recovered them at once, called them in unequivocally.

So far so good, since here was a probable source of what Mecron the black market held and not much chance that they could draw on it again. But there was a carton with

Henry Leggatt still and that was much more delicate. For Henry Leggatt. Of course he wouldn't part with it voluntarily, but these Cypriots were resourceful and Henry should be warned of it. That wasn't difficult in itself: what was difficult was Russell, for Charles Russell feared and hated Mecron. If he knew that a carton was in private hands still he'd insist on its security, putting it in a safe at least. And Henry was already compromised—unjustly but there it was. . . . Suspicion and the hint of worse, that bloody *Gong*. Any approach from Russell, the Security Executive of all people, at this of all moments. . . . Suppose it leaked. It wasn't impossible, not with *The Gong. The Gong*. . . .

Rachel shuddered, imagining the headlines. She'd have to warn Henry privately. She owed him that as she owed him much more.

Very deliberately she tore the report up. She could tell Russell all or nothing, for half the facts was always fatal, not worth its dangers. She put the pieces in her bag. Later she'd burn them.

She frowned in uncertainty. She'd have to warn Henry herself, and she was something more than hesitant. She hadn't seen him for sixteen years; he was married and, by all accounts, unhappily. It would be dangerous to stir things up again, and the danger would be hers.

But back at the Executive she went to Russell's office. She was on excellent terms with his secretary, for she had learnt that the keepers of kings' consciences weren't less important than the kings themselves. She asked her easily: 'What's he got fixed tonight?'

'Privately, you mean?'

'Yes—after hours.'

The secretary looked at a diary. 'He's going to a party at Lady Lampeter's.'

'I'd heard she had one.'

'Do you want to see him?'

'Yes, if he's free.'

'He'll be free to you.'

Rachel went in and Russell pulled a chair up. She didn't

57

beat about the bush. 'I've been prying into your private engagements, and you're going to Lady Lampeter's tonight. I'd like you to take me.'

'Whatever for?' Russell was clearly astonished. 'Molly Lampeter's a bitch, a politically ambitious one, though her whisky's impeccable. She's throwing one of her parties tonight and I'm a victim. Quite a willing one really: one hears things at parties. That is if you listen. But what on earth do you want to go for?'

'She's a great one for politicians.'

'She's that all right.'

'I'd like to meet one.'

'Yes? Any old politician?'

'Not any old politician. Henry Leggatt.'

'It's a fair chance he'll be there. Junior Ministers are very much her meat and I've seen him at Molly Lampeter's before.' There was a longish pause which Russell broke; finally he said quietly: 'I thought you already knew him.'

'That was a long time ago.'

'So it was. In the war, I think you told me.'

'Very much in the war.'

'You'd meet him again? I dare say you know how things are with him. Privately.'

She considered before she answered and Russell noticed it. Almost reluctantly she said: 'He's in trouble, you know. I really think I ought to.'

'I won't ask you for explanations. I gave you *carte blanche* and meant it.' Colonel Russell thought again. 'He's pretty certain to be there. I can check it in any case, and I'll speak to the Lampeter. But I think he'll be there.' He waited a second, then added smoothly: 'Possibly with his wife.' He was watching Rachel quietly as he said it.

Her face told him nothing, but he hadn't expected it. Rachel Borrodaile had been trained in a hard school. She said impersonally: 'You'll take me then? You'll have me introduced?'

'I'll take you with pleasure.'

For an instant she hesitated again. 'I'll go,' she said at last.

'I'll call for you at half past six.'

'I'll be ready.'

Russell walked to the door with her. As she went past him she heard him mumble, and mumbling wasn't a vice of his. She asked surprised: 'What's that?'

For a moment Charles Russell looked embarrassed, and that was something she had seldom seen. He coughed; recovered himself. In his ordinary voice he said: 'You're a very good soldier.'

'Is that all I am?' Her smile was a little wry,

'No—no indeed. Till half past six.'

Rachel and Charles Russell arrived at Lady Lampeter's at the height of the party, for Rachel had given Russell a drink en route. The room was alive with the background roar of any successful cocktail party in vigorous middle age—talk at its banal worst or, in an occasional corner, surprisingly good. These pockets of rare mutual enjoyment Molly Lampeter mistrusted, breaking them up ruthlessly. She writhed through the mill, panting a little, an expensive scent competing with teeth not quite beyond suspicion. Her man-servant stood apart, brooding on better days, and white-coated waiters from North London fought through the crowd with trays and what they imagined were Italian accents.

It was one of Lady Lampeter's parties.

Russell and Rachel Borrodaile were announced into a din where nobody could have caught their names, and Molly Lampeter shook hands with them. She always shook hands. 'But Charles! Too sweet of you to come.' She swivelled on Rachel gushingly. 'And this is your girl friend.'

'I wish it were,' he said.

'Too nice of you to come.'

Rachel smiled politely. 'Too nice of you to let me.'

They slipped away quietly as a man from the Foreign Office was announced in turn. He was trying not to look patronizing in company which he considered a thought below his present station. He had been born in Bognor. Russell took two whiskies from a passing tray, sniffing them quickly. He had said that the Lampeter whisky was impeccable, but he was cautious by instinct as well as training, and he valued his digestion. The sniff had been very expert, almost unnoticeable unless you had been looking for it, but it had reassured Charles Russell. He handed a glass to Rachel. 'Quite safe. Put it down and I'll scrounge another.' His smile was mischievous. 'I dare say you're going to need it.'

They stood quietly, looking around them, but Molly Lampeter was on them almost at once. She said to Rachel in her carefully home-counties voice: 'There's a friend of yours here, a very old friend. He's dying to meet you again.'

'Really?'

'Yes really. *Dying* to meet you, dear. It seems you were in the war together. France. Something terribly exciting.'

'It was frightening, yes.'

'Well, come along.'

Henry was standing by the fireplace, for an instant alone, and Lady Lampeter led Rachel up to him. For a moment he stared at her. 'Rachel,' he said.

Rachel had smiled, but it had cost her an effort. Henry, she thought, looked terrible. It had been sixteen years, of course—she could count them—and Henry must be in his middle forties. But he wasn't wearing them gracefully. She had told Charles Russell that he was the type to take care of himself. It didn't offend her to have been wrong, but she was shocked just how wrong she had been. Henry was soft, his face was puffy. And he looked desperately tired. Rachel managed to say casually: 'How are you, Henry?'

'Fine.'

She didn't believe him. Physically he looked all in, and there was something as well, a more than physical malaise.

You learnt a great deal about a man when you were on the run with him. A fortnight it had been, fourteen long days with the Gestapo never more than a jump behind them.

At the end it had been none.

She said, making her voice sound normal: 'How's that burn?'

'You can still see the scar.' For the first time he smiled a smile she recognized. 'I'll show you some time.'

'Some other place,' she said.

'And how's that foot of yours?'

'Oh, not too bad. At first they gave me a wooden one—damned clumsy thing. Now I've gone modern—springs and a sort of cantilever. It's most ingenious. I can walk almost naturally.' She waved her foot in its superlative shoe. 'Look.'

'Some other place.'

They laughed together, easily, the years slipping from them. Henry went for another whisky, offering it without fuss, saying in a voice which she knew was more than social: 'You're looking very well. You've changed, of course, but not a lot.' For a moment he hesitated. 'You're a beautiful woman still.'

'Steel foot and all?'

'Iron foot and all of it.'

She didn't return the compliment for she couldn't face the lie. He looked near to his physical limit. Politics must be hell: they sucked your viscera, took all of you. They were worth it, she supposed, if you were really a runner; they were worth it if you started from inside. Henry hadn't an earthly. Henry was a gentleman in waiting. She owed her life to a gentleman in waiting.

She wondered whether he had sensed the trap. . . . No, or he would hardly have left Hassertons. He had been doing very well in Hassertons, he'd have left them only from a sense of real vocation. She looked at him without appearing to. Rachel had lived amongst clever men for a good many years, and now cleverness wasn't something to which she attached great importance. It was a gift—oh yes, it was a gift; but it wasn't a virtue.

'And how do you like politics?'

'They keep me damned busy.'

She could see that he spoke the truth. Six years in the mill, she decided, and now—now Parliamentary Secretary to a ministry which was really the party's public relations office. At the taxpayer's expense. He spoke very well and he was splendid on T.V. So they used him remorselessly. He was an image, a convenient front for what didn't exist, the new man in the party, neither rich nor connected, the middle-class man of talent, rising on pure merit, rising. . . .

Rising to Parliamentary Secretary to the Ministry of Social Welfare.

And that would be the lot.

On an impulse she couldn't resist Rachel asked suddenly: 'And how's your wife?'

'She isn't here tonight.'

No, Rachel thought, she wouldn't be. A party at Molly Lampeter's would hardly attract an Egham. Eghams might accept things but they wouldn't work for them. The Eghams were a great political clan, the marquess its most honourable apex. Eghams were in—right in. Eghams were in by birth. Not that Henry would have married her for that.

That made it worse.

'Another whisky?' Henry spoke comfortably, much more relaxed. A drink or two had helped him, eased him too obviously. Rachel mistrusted it. 'Well. . . .'

'Oh come on.'

Henry returned with the whisky, passing it almost masterfully. 'And how do *you* do?'

'I've got a job.'

'I gathered you didn't need one.'

'I still need to work.'

'All right—what work?'

'I'm in something called the Security Executive.'

She saw his face change. Faces often did change when you told them you worked in the Security Executive, but Rachel was observant and the change in Henry Leggatt's hadn't been wholly defensive. He repeated reflectively: 'The Security Executive?'

'Yes.' Rachel nodded at Charles Russell in a corner. 'That's my boss. Do you know him?'

'Only by reputation. Everybody knows Charles Russell by reputation.' He seemed to be thinking it over. 'You're his secretary?'

'No.'

She saw him flush but helped him. 'As it happens I'm fairly senior.'

'All that stuff in the war?'

'That helped, I suppose. But I'm very respectable now. I'm a desk hand.'

He said thoughtfully, turning the words over: 'The Security Executive?'

'Yes.'

'It sounds—well, secure.'

'I think I could guarantee that.'

'Rachel, will you dine with me?'

Somehow she wasn't surprised. 'Of course.'

She could see him considering again, but he'd seldom thought fast. At last he said: 'Do you go out of London at week-ends?'

'Never unless I have to. I hate the country.'

'My wife does, nearly always. Could you manage Sunday?'

'I'd like to.'

Lady Lampeter was inching towards them. They seemed to be getting on very well, and it was a principle of Lady Lampeter's to part any couple which seemed to be getting on very well. Besides, a Minister, even a junior Minister, was something of a lion; he could be used; passed around; exhibited. Molly Lampeter said breathily: 'Henry. . . .'

'Till Sunday then.'

Lady Lampeter led him away to boredom and Rachel collected her fur. At the door Charles Russell was awaiting her. His expression was inscrutable, but she knew him too well to imagine that much had missed him. Nothing in fact. Charles Russell said blandly: 'I'll get you a taxi.'

'I'd much rather walk.'

Dr. Hugh Latta lived in a modern maisonette in St. John's Wood. He lived mostly alone, but he had an efficient daily housekeeper. He ate at the Mandarins, and this evening he had returned from an indifferent dinner intending to work on the reports on Mecron. They had begun to pile up, both those from his own laboratory and others from Cambridge, where he had asked colleagues to co-operate. This hadn't been solely a passion for truth, an emotion which in Latta ran less strongly than in many scientists. On the contrary he had considered Cambridge useful. Whatever his final decision a discreet reference to Cambridge would be helpful to it. It would be a selective reference, naturally. Latta wouldn't have admitted that any laboratory at Cambridge had a higher prestige than his own, but he was prepared to use the name. When it suited his conclusions.

As he turned the key he knew at once that something was wrong. The front door led, through a little vestibule for coats, direct into the sitting-room, and the sitting-room was grave-yard cold. That wasn't like his housekeeper at all. He turned on the light and blinked. The cold was at once explained, for the window was wide open. And, final outrage, his desk was in chaos. Reports and graphs, beautifully drawn, a mass of unfiled paper, strewed the floor.

He moved to the window quickly. A man was climbing from the basement well. Hugh Latta shouted but the man didn't turn his head. He completed his climb, leisurely but expert, over the railing and into the street. For a moment he stood unmoving, his back to Latta, his right hand deep in his pocket. Then he turned suddenly.

Dr. Latta was against the light. He didn't consider it, but Hugh Latta was a sitting duck.

For an instant the intruder hesitated. Latta couldn't see his face, for over the eyes a wide-brimmed hat was pulled well down and over the mouth a scarf well up. The man stood motionless, apparently weighing a decision he hadn't expected. Latta shouted again. The man didn't answer him. He seemed to be listening, and Latta, by reflex, listened too.

Yes, there was a taxi turning into the cul-de-sac.

The stranger shrugged, then started to run lightly, past the discharging taxi.

Dr. Latta rang the police and, while they were arriving, searched the maisonette. Nothing had been taken and he had quite a few things worth stealing. He smiled in satisfaction.

Some miserable thief, he thought—another ten minutes at the Mandarins, the brandy he'd refused, and the wretch would have got away with it. In a drawer of the desk there was over thirty pounds. He'd missed even that.

Dr. Hugh Latta decided he'd been lucky.

As indeed he had.

8

CHARLES RUSSELL WAS walking back to the Security
Executive from the excellent lunch which Rachel Borrodaile
had advised him to buy George Clee. He walked with a long,
a faintly ceremonial stride, his hard hat straight over bright
blue eyes. It was drizzling lightly, but not enough to tempt
him to disturb a meticulously rolled umbrella. He walked in
abstraction, thinking, for he had plenty to think about.
Russell had been generous with wine and brandy, though he
hadn't expected that a drink or two, a civilized if ample meal,
would do more to George Clee than gently mellow him. Nor
had it done so. Over a second brandy, an admirable claret
already inside him, he had been as correct and as cautious as
over the sherry. He had been cautious and correct, even a little
dour, but he had perfectly communicated his opinion of Hugh
Latta. Russell wasn't a scientist, he was a stranger to Clee's
world, but he hadn't expected him to foul a private nest. But
though Clee had said nothing positive he was an artist at the
thing unsaid. Silences, half a smile, the question turned not
met—these had told Russell as clearly as words that Clee's
opinion of Latta wasn't a high one. Latta wasn't wholly to be
trusted, or not by another scientist; Latta was ambitious,
mightn't be too scrupulous, and Latta was a disappointed
man.

Charles Russell, swinging his umbrella, frowned. It had
been Lord Acton, he remembered, who had tossed off the
aphorism that all power corrupts, absolute power corrupts
absolutely. It was a splendid generalization, true, more than
likely, when power had been something which could be
identified, an attribute vested in a few score hands. But today
it simply wasn't. Today it wasn't power which corrupted: it

was management. All management corrupts and absolute management corrupts absolutely.

Moreover management bred its own diseases. In the Establishment, for instance, though the word was irritating to a fastidious mind. Russell couldn't remember hearing it before the war except in the context of the dreariest division of Staff Duties, but today it was a cliché. It was a target for angry men, one distressingly easy to hit. But assuming it meant anything at all the Establishment had one thing in common with the men who formed it: the Establishment collectively, like the individuals it devoured, was heir to precise diseases.

Blindness was one of them. Charles Russell shrugged. Condemnation didn't come easily to him, and moreover he knew the stresses. The machine grew more complex yearly, more rapacious of the men who served it. Moloch. Only to keep it going, never to look up, never to ask where or why. Into its limitless maw went friends and family, an intelligent man's interests, his life. You could never forget it and you could never sit still. Its servants were half janissary, half blinded slave. At fifty they were flabby and at sixty it pensioned them. Shortly they died. *Digne puer meliore flamma*—that was Martial, wasn't it? Russell smiled, pleased that he could remember a little Latin. It wasn't in fashion but nor was he.

So it wasn't extraordinary that the second disease of this extraordinary world was one of values. How they coveted the symbols that they hadn't lost ground, the two or three letters after their names, the sadly depreciated handle to precede it. Russell couldn't understand it; he had genuinely never been tempted by honours. He was an Anglo-Irishman, and though he could tell himself by now that he had mastered the social intricacies of the English professional class he had never accepted its symbols of status. He had a decoration himself, one which he had won in battle; he would have admitted that he was proud of it. But the other kind, something that came with the rations, an acknowledgement that you were level with the rats your contemporaries, twenty or forty years of miraculous mediocrity. . . .

No, no, and no.

67

But though Russell had never been tempted he knew just how potent the temptation was. Steal a man's life, mew him up in Whitehall or some sprawling corporation, filch from him sun and leisure, women, a Mediterranean sea. . . .

Naturally he'd seek substitutes, unconsciously he'd look for reassurance. He'd find it, in time, in the machine itself. The machine had destroyed him but he mustn't be unrecognized.

Charles Russell considered Latta against this background, and he would have confessed it frightened him. Latta was head of a famous laboratory, but Latta wasn't up with the gang. He wasn't Sir Hugh. It didn't matter why—some slip perhaps, some enemy made unknowingly. And he had nothing outside his work. He wasn't married, he lived alone; he even ate at the Mandarins. A thin life, Russell thought it, poor, unrewarding. And thinking of rewards again. . . .

Dr. Latta was a scientist, or to be accurate an eminent scientific administrator. But Dr. Latta was unrecognized, or at least unrecognized by the standards of his fellow Mandarins. And Dr. Latta was conducting an inquiry into Mecron, with which was involved a Minister—just possibly, if things went wrong, the government itself—with which, in whose hands, whose gift. . . .

Back in the Security Executive Russell unlocked a safe. He took from it a police report on an unsuccessful burglary at Latta's maisonette. He had let it be known that he had an unspecified interest in Dr. Hugh Latta, and when Russell disclosed an official interest it was surprising how much paper would come in to him. He read the report again. It was a routine, a perfectly neutral police report. An intruder had been interrupted by Dr. Hugh Latta himself, apparently in the act of rifling his desk. Some confidential papers had been disturbed but nothing had been taken. There were no finger-prints, and the window had been cut, not forced. It looked a professional job. Dr. Latta had seen the thief but he wouldn't be able to recognize him again. The police were far from hopeful.

Charles Russell sent for Rachel Borrodaile. He had a precise

68

and logical mind, but he was a very good security officer and, after a certain point, he mistrusted both logic and precision. It was his opinion that they were the occupational vices of all officials. After a time experience displaced intelligence: something called judgément rose as the sacred cow. Russell couldn't have defined it but it often made the stupidest mistakes. But Rachel Borrodaile was still a woman. Her logic wasn't as sharp as Russell's, but one expositor was plenty. She had something instead and Russell respected it.

She came in quietly and he put her into the armchair, passing her the police report. She read it deliberately before she commented.

'Dr. Latta seems to have been lucky.'

'You think so?'

'Don't you?'

'But I was asking *you*.' Colonel Russell was his blandest.

She thought it over carefully, for she knew Charles Russell. He never charged his fences, he could be maddening, but there was method in his madness. At length she said: 'You're certainly creeping up on it—stalking the thing. But I've the ghost of an inkling what you're getting at.'

'Good. But hold it a minute while I spell it out.' Russell began to do so. 'Either this was a burglary or it was not. You can agree with that?'

Rachel couldn't help laughing. 'Yes.'

But Russell wasn't offended. 'So that if it was a burglary, Latta disturbed the burglar. Nothing was taken. Then Latta, as you said, was lucky.'

She nodded solemnly, unsmiling now.

'But if it wasn't a burglary the fact that nothing was taken wouldn't be relevant. In which case nor would luck.'

'Granted,' she said. It wasn't the first time she'd played this game with Russell.

Charles Russell sat back. 'Then it's your turn to think.'

She did so for some time, for Russell would pounce on slips, saying at last: 'Latta's papers were on the floor. The preliminary stuff on Mecron, but quite a lot of it.'

'Which an ordinary burglar might have thrown there try-

69

ing to break into the desk, or which a very unordinary burglar might have been examining.'

'It's a hypothesis,' she said. She'd acquired the word from Russell.

'Do you dispute it?'

'No.'

For the first time he laughed. 'You'd better not. It was you who had the pricking of the thumbs about Hugh Latta.'

She returned it in an instant. 'And it was you who insisted that the one thing the Cypriots wouldn't want would be for Mecron to be found harmless.'

'This burglar, then. Putting two and two together—'

'I make them five,' she said.

'Five is sometimes right. In the Security Executive.'

There was a reflective silence which Rachel broke. She seemed to be changing the subject. 'Have you met Clee yet?'

'I've just been having lunch with him. He helped a lot; he gave me a very clear picture.' Russell repeated it precisely, and Rachel whistled. 'Go on,' Russell said.

'I was thinking that that sort of reputation, that sort of human smell. . . .'

'It's difficult to hide. It does leak around.'

'But outside a man's own world? Outside, in this case, scientific circles?'

Russell said judicially: 'If anyone outside the world of scientists needed an estimate of Latta's private character I don't think they'd find it difficult to get.'

'Our friends, for instance?'

'Our friends for certain. We're agreed they've a motive. If Latta is something short of scrupulous, if Latta is even suspect of playing politics with Mecron, personal politics, finding it's harmless when it's not. . . .'

'I might not wish to be Hugh Latta. I told you our friends aren't innocents.'

'I didn't contradict you. If Mecron is found innocuous, whatever the motive of the man who does so, bang go their prospects of handling a dangerous drug since there won't by definition be a dangerous drug to handle. But we're assuming the thing *is* dangerous. Moreover we're assuming that these people think so too. So that if it's corruptive and isn't declared so, by Latta, for private reasons, if they think that's a possibility. . . .'

'Should I put a man on Latta? Someone to keep an eye on him?'

'If I knew he was straight I'd say yes at once. That would be a duty.'

'But as it is?'

Russell didn't answer directly. 'Hugh Latta takes papers home. That's probably quite in order since they're papers from his own laboratory. But by now he'll be locking them up.' He glanced again at the police report. 'There's a safe, I see, though it hadn't been touched.'

'I'd give plenty to see Latta's papers.'

'I'd spend my own money to do so. Mecron could be hell.' Russell was emphatic but he wasn't encouraging. 'There's a safe,' he repeated.

'There's a safe.'

They sat in total silence for perhaps three minutes. Rachel was thinking and Russell waited. At last he asked, deliberately formal: 'Do you wish to consult me?'

'Do I need orders?'

He laughed again. 'Not very often.'

She rose and Russell with her. At the door he said casually: 'You'll pick a good man, of course.'

'Oh yes, I'll pick a good one.'

Rachel went back to her room, but not at once to work. Instead she walked to the mirror. . . . Good skin, nice hair, a splendid figure still. It wouldn't be self-deception if she told herself she didn't look thirty-six. That was the score, though.

She returned to her desk, hating it suddenly. She'd sat at a desk for years, this or another, and now she was pretty senior. She was a senior security officer, its technique at her fingertips, but she had lost her personal skills. Perhaps that was essential middle age—losing your skills. The cotton wool came down on you, experience and authority, the power to give others orders, instructions which you couldn't carry out. Not for yourself, for you had lost your skills. . . . She sat at a desk, noting, digesting, putting up the important ones. At thirty-six years of age.

She began to laugh quietly. What she was considering was nothing now, a mere peccadillo. Her boats were burnt already. She'd torn a report up, suppressed information, concealed from her superior something he wished to know.

She picked up the telephone, asking for a nursing home in Wimbledon.

She wasn't feeling ill.

Russell had engaged himself for what he would have called an old friends' evening, since he had known the Erskines for most of his life. Tim Erskine had served in the same regiment. He hadn't been brilliant but he had been a competent officer; he had retired exactly when Russell would have expected him to retire—three years command and finish. He had been a year or two junior to Russell himself, but they had always been friendly. And Mary Erskine he admired. In the difficult vocation of wife of a regimental officer she had been conspicuously successful. Besides, he liked her personally. Tim Erskine had taken his pension and, without much difficulty, had found himself a not too distinguished job. He had always been sensible and he hadn't expected the earth. He hadn't secured it but he had resettled himself respectably. Russell admired that too.

He rang the bell of the Erskines' flat with a pleasant sense of anticipation. It was going to be an evening: they were going to let their hair down. They'd talk shop, old campaigns and regimental gossip. It would bore clever people, but that didn't mean that it wouldn't be enjoyable. . . . Charlie Watters and that mule team. Pity the Japs got him. And what happened to Monica? Married again? Well, she'd been a smasher. And sport—shooting in India. Not the kind where Personages sat in a wired *machan*, shooting at driven animals, half doped, through telescopic sights and rifles which would stop a tank. But *sport*. No elephants, no dreadful *bundobast*, not murder. You took a Mannlicher and off you went. A dozen friendly beaters as anxious for fun as you were. Off you all went and sometimes you all came back again.

So Russell rang the Erskines' bell agreeably certain of entertainment. Mary Erskine admitted him, and at once he knew that something was amiss. The room was warm and drinks had been set out—Mary Erskine on her deathbed wouldn't fail in hospitality—but clearly she was on edge. She gave him a gin but she wasn't at ease; she said in a voice he'd never heard: 'Tim isn't ready yet.'

'Tell him he needn't hurry.'

'He can't.'

Russell sat silently, grey, wise and approachable. Finally he asked easily: 'One over the eight?' They were very old friends and Tim Erskine had had his failings, modest and never serious failings, but he had sometimes hugged the bottle.

'I wish to God it were.'

She began to cry quietly but in a desperation which only a fool would have missed. It shattered Russell. He had never seen her cry, nor thought of Mary crying. But he knew her too well to risk a facile comfort: instead he let her cry, five minutes perhaps, then, as she recovered herself, choosing his moment, Russell said simply: 'Tell me.'

She looked at him, hesitating. 'You're a very old friend but I'm a very bad hostess.'

'Forget about the hostess.'

'You're sure?"

'Of course I'm sure. I'm an old, old soldier, but I've an old sweat's privileges.'

'Then have you heard of Mecron?'

'As it happens I have.'

'It's a tranquillizer.'

'So they say.'

She looked at him unhappily. 'You've heard things too, then?'

Russell nodded.

'Then I'm not just a silly woman. Mecron. . . .' She started to cry again; checked herself grimly. 'Tim's on the Mecron.'

'*On* it?'

'It's got him hopelessly.'

It came out rather slowly, in hesitations, rushes, the reticences of a self-respecting woman talking about misfortune. . . . The difficult time at the office, uncertainty and extra work, the trusted subordinate who hadn't been quite so trustworthy. The friend who'd recommended Mecron. . . .

But Russell broke in gently. 'You know this friend?'

'Oh yes, quite well. He's a very nice man. He might almost be you.'

'Thank you. But I don't use Mecron.'

'He does. And that's about the word for it. *He* uses Mecron. It—it *serves* him. But Tim it's destroying. He's lying there now, drunk I'd have said if I didn't know he wasn't. In an hour he'll be wonderful, unnaturally, shamefully wonderful. That I could take as I've taken his occasional booze-ups. But this isn't occasional. Tomorrow he'll want it again, and tomorrow he'll take it. Tomorrow and the day after and the day after that.' Her voice broke miserably.

'Do you know where he buys it?'

'No.'

'There's none in the shops, you know.'

'I know it. They tell you some story about a delivery soon. Some breakdown at the factory.'

'Do you know if he stocked it up?'

'I'm quite sure he didn't.'

'Have you asked him where he gets it?'

'Yes.'

'What did he tell you?'

'He told me to go to hell.'

Russell rose slowly, taking her hand. She protested but not convincingly. 'You're sure you won't stay?' She looked at her wristwatch, her mouth twisting savagely. 'It's less than the full hour now.'

'I don't think I'll stay.'

'You're an awfully nice man.'

74

'An awfully useless one.'

Charles Russell found a taxi, directing it to his flat. He sat in it swearing softly. He had said he was useless and useless he felt. It wasn't a sensation he was accustomed to. And there was another even more unfamiliar. For a moment he hesitated, instinct warning him that once he recognized it he wouldn't much care for what he saw. But finally he faced it. It was commitment, a personal involvement, and Russell loathed it. Good officials didn't feel personal involvement—oughtn't to. Responsibility by all means; responsibility was a quiet thing, discipline under another name, but an official who felt privately was a very bad official, quite apart from the fact that to do so was a recipe for suicide. But Russell knew now that he hated Mecron, feared it. He felt about Mecron like. . . .

Like, he decided, that Peter Davis had. Bloody young fool. Russell could have thought of a dozen ways of bringing Mecron to a crisis much more delicate, much more effective than blurting a front-page story to *The Gong*. *The Gong* of all papers! Precipitate young fool. But now they were two of a kind. Russell smiled grimly. He'd have done it much better himself, but then he wasn't an Assistant Principal; he knew his Whitehall and he knew its ropes. So presently he'd use them and on Davis's behalf. But not at once, for that would be clumsy. Davis must take his medicine or at least one dose of it. But later, when the heat came off, Russell would get busy where it mattered. There mustn't be victimization, or not of a fellow victim. They were in this together, a young man's emotions generously given, an old one's reluctantly, hating it. But equally given.

At his flat he mixed himself a whisky, scratching in the icebox for the dinner he hadn't had. . . . Well, they were waiting on Latta: a look at Latta's papers was the next firm move. It was fortunate Rachel Borrodaile was competent. Russell wondered whom she would choose. An ordinary break-in man would be useless since he wouldn't know what to look for. He needn't be a scientist but he must be accustomed to papers. What they wanted wasn't the material itself but Latta's own notes on it, the way his mind was working. . . . Yes, he'd have to be rather a special man.

It was fortunate Miss Borrodaile chose well.

In Dick Asher's fashionably decorated flat the telephone rang sharply. He wasn't pleased for he had been asleep. He put on a dressing-gown which most men would have thought extravagant and went into the sitting-room.

'Dick Asher here.'

'I've been trying to report for days.'

'I've been out a lot—busy.'

'The fool came back early. He nearly caught me.'

'He didn't, though?'

'No. And I saw what we wanted.'

'And . . . ?'

'And it's bad. The technical stuff so far looks just about breaking even. Some of it points one way, some another. But he'd left some private notes on it, a sort of draft of a report.' For a moment the voice was silent, then said decidedly: 'He's going to sink us.'

'You're sure of it?'

'Quite sure. He means to cook it.'

Asher said quietly: 'He mustn't do that.'

He went back to make up sleep.

Rachel took a train to Wimbledon and then a bus. She could remember her way but not too well. She left the bus at a corner which she only just recognized, walking perhaps half a mile. On the right of a prosperous avenue was what was called common, to the left were solid and pompous houses. She found one she thought familiar and rang the bell. A courteous Negro explained that it was the embassy of a state which, three years ago, hadn't existed. Rachel tried another. It was the residence of a gentleman who had made a recent fortune by buying up flats in London and doubling the rents. Finally she found what she wanted. The notice was very

76

discreet and she didn't blame herself for missing it—*St. Justine's Nursing Home.*

She rang the bell again and a maid in uniform opened to her.

'I'd like to see matron, please.'

'I'm afraid matron's busy.' The maid was a little pert.

'Then I'll wait for her. Give her this card, please.' Rachel gave the maid the visiting card of Colonel Charles Russell. It was yellowing with age, curled at the corners.

The maid hesitated, but Rachel's manner was decisive. They went into the waiting-room and the maid slipped away. Rachel looked about her. It was a pleasant enough room but as impersonal as the grave. The flowers were arranged in the manner of a woman quite without feeling for them, but one who had taken an expensive course in flower arrangement. The periodicals were fresh. Rachel sat down to read one, making a mental note that if ever she were sick she would certainly look elsewhere. Presently matron appeared. She was a stiff, precise Scotswoman, and Rachel made a tick against her mental note. The matron said professionally: 'Can I help you?'

'You have my card, I think.'

The matron frowned. 'But I don't think I know you.'

'The card admits.'

'I know. But still. . . .'

'You're right to be careful. May I ask how long you've been here?'

'I've been here five years.'

'I haven't been here for that and more.'

The matron looked at the card in her hand. 'It's pretty old,' she said.

'I know it is.'

'You haven't anything else, I suppose? No—no identification?'

'I've this,' Rachel said. She opened her bag, looking at matron not into it, and an astonished matron was staring at a workmanlike Luger. At, but not down, for Rachel Borrodaile had been properly trained with firearms. The matron

77

said quickly: 'I see,' and Rachel put the gun away. They climbed into a little lift and up four floors. At the top of the house was a landing and a single door. 'You can find your own way out again?' Matron was being sarcastic.

'Thank you, I can.'

The matron took the lift again and Rachel knocked on the door. A judas she'd forgotten opened alarmingly, and a lean brown face was inspecting her. For a moment it looked blank, then split in a welcoming grin.

'Why, Miss Rachel.'

'Why, Mr. Lightlove.'

'Call me Charlie—you always used to.' Charlie opened the door, shutting it behind Rachel carefully. 'This *is* a surprise.'

'I'm a little surprised myself.'

'Come to knock off a few? A Luger, wasn't it?'

'I've not come to shoot.'

'A pity. You were bloody good. Come and see what we've got, though. There've been changes.' He led the way into a long gallery, switching on a light to do so since it was windowless, pointing at the walls and floor. 'Wonderful new stuff they've given us—fibreglass or something. The bods downstairs are all T.B. I don't think they sleep much, but they wouldn't hear a field gun.'

'I had a bit of bother getting in.'

'You did? I'm glad of that. Matron's a bitch but she knows her stuff. This place is much too valuable to risk. The cover's almost perfect.' Mr. Lightlove grinned again. 'Now just a bang or two for old time's sake. There's a gun in that bag of yours. I smell it.'

'I'm not on a shooting job.'

'What *are* you on?'

She told him quickly.

'Well, well. You've done it, of course—I don't deny it. But it was some time ago.'

'So was the shooting. So was that stuff with the garotte.'

'You were an expert with that.'

'And with locks I'm not?'

'I didn't say that, though it's partly what I meant. You were

78

good, I admit it, but it wasn't your speciality.' For an instant Mr. Lightlove was almost pleading. 'Now wouldn't a man of our own. . . .'

'I don't want a man of our own.'

Charlie Lightlove shrugged resignedly. 'You're the boss.' He was suddenly decided. 'It's a safe, I suppose?'

'There's a safe, though I may not have to touch it if I'm lucky.'

'What sort of a safe?'

'A pushover.'

'How do you know?'

'The police told us that. The police have been in the place, though for perfectly normal reasons, and they noticed the safe. It's one of those silly wall things, and years and years pre-war. A decent modern cashbox would be a whole lot harder. The front door worries me much more. It's right on the street and the lock's a good one.'

'Which lock?'

She told him again.

'What year?'

'Forty-seven or forty-eight.'

'You're sure?'

'I've cased it.'

'Good. Lucky it isn't forty-nine. By forty-nine they'd tightened it considerable.' Mr. Lightlove reflected. 'You're sure you don't want a man?'

'I'm sure.'

'All right then, I'll take you to Ben. He's rising eighty and three parts blind, but he's still the best craftsman living." They began to walk along a corridor. 'Second door on the left, and don't mention his beard. Half of it's in some lock still, some patent they said would fox him. It didn't, though.'

9

MR. ROBERT SENESCHAL was in an indifferent temper.
He considered that the Home Secretary had handled it badly
in the House and that he himself could have managed the
whole thing better. The Question about Mecron hadn't been
a destructive one: on the contrary it had been carefully
drafted not to be destructive. But what followed the first
Question was what mattered, and it was Seneschal's opinion
that the Home Secretary had been much below proper form.
Perhaps he was getting old. So much the better for Seneschal.

Robert Seneschal would have admitted that the position
hadn't been easy. One shocking sore thumb stuck out, the
horn on a political sea mine. The ordinary man would ask
one thing: if something was wrong with Mecron, even suspected to be wrong, why wasn't it simply prohibited until
officially cleared or otherwise?

Seneschal smiled thinly. It was an ordinary man's question,
and for the ordinary man's questions he had the intellectual's
contempt. The questions of ordinary men were always over-
simplified. Nevertheless Seneschal could imagine the flap in
the Home Office. It would have gone to the lawyers at once,
and the lawyers would have had a field day. It wouldn't have
been a case of one saying one thing and one another: on the
contrary they would have been unanimous—unanimous in
pointing out the difficulties, then delicately ducking them.
And of course it *was* tricky. For here was something called
Mecron, a handful of orthodox chemicals plus one biochemical which at least wasn't known to be noxious. The
evidence that Mecron was dangerous was popular evidence if
it was evidence at all. Powers to take action apart (and the
lawyers would have been cautious about powers) it would be
something very serious to throw a product of Hassertons at

a government laboratory. The lawyers would have shivered.
. . . Even if powers existed, it wouldn't be inconceivable that
an action in the Courts. . . .

There wasn't a precedent for Mecron, and a lawyer without a precedent was a very unhappy animal. Even a good
one. A departmental lawyer, one who didn't have to earn a
living in the competitive world of lawyers—a departmental
lawyer without a precedent would quite simply be useless.
He'd record the pros and cons; bat the ball back to his
Minister. By his own dim lights he would have done his duty.

There were difficulties undeniably, but unhappily they
weren't an answer, or not outside Whitehall; they weren't an
answer to the ordinary man's question, and they hadn't been
an answer to an Opposition smelling blood. And the Home
Secretary had played a difficult hand badly. There was only
one technique when you were hiding something—indecision
for instance: you must somehow convey that you were all in
this together, that there was nothing you would like better
than the support of the House, your colleagues, your equals
before the electorate. You'd love to lean on them, to share.
Only some rule, some stupid technicality prevented you.

It nearly always worked, for the House wasn't less susceptible to flattery than the men who sat in it. It was a trick but
it worked. Seneschal had seen it used a hundred times, often
by the Home Secretary himself. But yesterday he'd done the
worst thing possible. His words had been unexceptionable
but his manner ministerial. Somehow he'd implied a fatal
superiority; somehow he'd contrived the impression that a
fool of a backbencher hadn't the *right* to know. When he'd
been a Minister, something he never would be, he'd understand these things.

The Home Secretary had had a very rough passage, and
Seneschal wasn't surprised. Even the arrangement with the
Templeton laboratory hadn't saved him. It was part of an
answer at least and, with the lawyers scuttling to a lawyer's
traditional cover, not at all a bad one. On another day and
in another man's mouth it might have worked and well. But
the Home Secretary had been inexplicably hamhanded. He

had announced the arrangement—that was the word, announced it; he had sounded self-satisfied, almost, Seneschal thought sardonically, as though he'd thought of it himself. But it hadn't gone down at all. There'd been a palpable smell of fish: worse, there'd been that electric little ripple through both sides of a hitherto two-party House.

A Minister was hiding something.

The Home Secretary had been saved by the bell, but he'd left the ring distinctly groggy. Seneschal was too experienced to suppose they'd leave it there. Sometime there'd be another round, sometime and somewhere. Seneschal couldn't guess when, but he began to consider it, thinking how he could turn it to his own advantage. He was Minister of Social Welfare and he ought to be Home Secretary. At least. And the Home Secretary had muffed one—quite a high ball at that. If he, Robert Seneschal, could somehow recover it. . . . But not too soon, of course. You got no thanks for stepping in too soon, and certainly no advancement. He'd have to time it sensibly, let it get worse, oh yes, a good deal worse. It wasn't enough that the Home Secretary was embarrassed: the party must be in it too. He must wait till it was serious, just short of crisis, then. . . .

His secretary came in quietly. 'The Prime Minister has been telephoning, sir. He'd like a word with you.'

'When did he say?'

'He said today if possible.'

'What are my engagements?'

'You've a Dr. Hugh Latta at noon.'

'Ask Number Ten if three will suit them.'

. . . By God it's coming quickly.

Robert Seneschal looked at his watch. There were ten minutes to midday still and he spent them thinking. . . . Dr. Hugh Latta of the Templeton laboratory. He'd asked for an interview and that had been interesting. Now it was something more. He was a scientist but he was also Hugh Latta. There were possibilities in Hugh Latta, immediate possibilities. Seneschal smiled his most Common Room smile. He mustn't be precise, of course: that would be most improper and it would probably scare Latta, but he flattered himself that he wasn't without resources. The thing unsaid, the mandarin's smile for a fellow Mandarin, the inference, delicate but, thinking it over later, obvious. The promise unmade but somehow accepted. . . .

He thought himself good at those.

Mr. Robert Seneschal was a man who had read everything which he considered worth attention, but the views of an early nineteenth-century official on statesmanship he wouldn't have thought useful. For instance, Henry Taylor's advice on Interviews:

2nd. All applicants for interviews should be required to send in on the day preceding that on which they are appointed to attend, a paper setting forth, as definitely as may be, the object which they seek and the facts which they have to state, with exact notes of reference to the dates of any correspondence which may have previously taken place upon the subject in question, and a *précis* of such correspondence.

3rd. A Minister would do well to have placarded in his ante-chamber a notice in the following or some similar form:—'Owing to the many inconveniences which have arisen to the public from oral communications being misunderstood or incorrectly remembered, A.B. thinks it his duty to apprise those who may do him the honour to attend him upon business, that he will in no case hold himself, his colleagues, or his successors, bound by words spoken, unless they shall have been subsequently reduced to writing and authenticated in that form.'

This matchless counsel Robert Seneschal had never stumbled on. If he had done so it would have struck him as cynical, and certainly as out of date. Robert Seneschal thought himself much too skilled at interviews to need the grassroots schooling of a Victorian civil servant. He would have resented Sir Henry Taylor; he wouldn't have read him respectfully.

83

And perhaps he would have been right. It was certain that Henry Taylor couldn't have dealt with Latta as did Seneschal. Probably he wouldn't have wished to, since he was an honourable man. He couldn't have sent him striding from his office, swinging his umbrella, trying not to hum in public, looking in plate-glass windows at a familiar reflection. Familiar but in some way different. . . . Sir Hugh. The man who'd done that splendid work on Mecron.

If that was the way they wanted it.

It suited the future Sir Hugh.

Rachel Borrodaile was changing her clothes deliberately, a familiar excitement rising in her belly. It was the needle. She would have admitted the emotion wasn't unpleasant—there were more sorts of drug than tranquillizers—and, in the moment of clarity preceding action, she would have conceded something more. She would have admitted that she had been deceiving herself. It was true that she had sat at a desk for far too long; it was true that she was losing her personal and hard-won skills; it was even true that Russell had given her *carte blanche*, though whatever he had meant by that it was certain he hadn't meant this. Nor tearing a report up. Russell would have been furious if he had known of either, and perfectly justifiably. But Rachel knew now that it wasn't Russell she was considering. Henry Leggatt was in trouble and she owed him her life.

She'd leave it for the moment that she owed him her life. On Sunday she was dining with him and. . . .

She checked her thoughts sharply, reviewing the evening before her. It was the little things that let you down, the getting there and back again, the not being seen. Hugh Latta lived alone, and it was known he worked late. No action would be even reasonable much before half past two, and it was most of four miles from Knightsbridge to St. John's Wood. Public transport wouldn't be running and a taxi was out of the question. She would have liked to walk but didn't dare chance it. Not with that foot of hers—not even in sensible shoes. She would have to take her car, but she'd had leisure to plan in detail.

In her time in the Resistance Rachel had heard a good many military clichés. Some had been merely banal, some, for the Resistance, actively dangerous. But one had stuck with her: time spent in reconnaissance is seldom wasted. And she had made her reconnaissance thoroughly, finding a street near Latta's, not too close but not too far, where night-parking was considerable. She regretted that her car was easily identifiable, a neat cream Giuliétta, but the bobby on the beat would see a hundred parked cars a night. That is, if there were a bobby on the beat. Hiring would be too danger-ous. She'd have to risk the Giulietta.

It was outside now as she made her final check. . . . A nondescript hat and nondescript clothes, the clothes of a respectable housewife returning, perhaps, from visiting a sick mother. She'd have got her to sleep at last. Rachel looked in her bag. . . . Gloves, thin and pliant, a good German flash-light with brand-new batteries, Ben's beautiful picklock. No gun. Guns were for amateurs, or fools.

Unless you really meant to use one. Short of the clear intention to take life guns were an embarrassment, and Rachel hadn't a motive to kill. Her plan if she were interrupted was perfectly simple: she'd run for it, foot and all. Foot and all she'd be faster than a middle-aged scientist over the two hundred yards to her car. She wasn't afraid of being caught and held. Hugh Latta was sixty and more, and she hadn't forgotten her unarmed combat. Once you had been good at it, it wasn't a thing you did forget. She had heavy horn glasses with lenses which were not, and clothes quite un-typical. Latta had never met her; Latta, if he saw her, might be able to describe; he might even describe in detail. So much the better since the detail would be misleading. There were risks still and she knew them, but they weren't the sort of risk which foresight could eliminate. She'd done her thinking, testing it against experience. The rest would be luck and she said a little prayer to it.

Rachel looked at her watch. It was two-fifteen precisely.

She climbed into her car, starting it quietly, slipping smoothly through the gears. She drove without hesitation, for she had twice made the journey, and at night. That was the sort of detail well worth checking.

Rachel had checked it.

She came to the street where she meant to leave the Giulietta. There were a dozen cars already but plenty of space still. Rachel parked her own on the left-hand side, locking the wheels outwards. That was detail again. She took the ignition key but did not lock the door.

She looked round quickly as she left the car, slipping away silently on rubber-soled shoes. There wasn't a soul in sight. She walked twice past Hugh Latta's maisonette, once in each direction. It told her nothing, or only the negative. There wasn't a light.

She went up six steps, conscious that her heart was thumping, a little ashamed of it. . . . Well, it had been many years, too many years. . . .

Rachel opened her bag. This was the hard part, for Ben had been frank with her. On what she could tell him he could give her a dozen keys—two dozen keys, a hundred. The odds were that one would fit, and blow what the makers said, but undeniably there were odds still. And trying would take time, time on an open doorstep. Moreover as the seconds ticked away a woman—a man for that—grew careless. Sooner or later there'd be noise. That was human and inevitable. Ben had shaken his untidy white head, staring at Rachel through enormous glasses. . . . On the other hand he had a little thing here which would open any lock of the make in question. *Any* lock of the make in question. Unfortunately it was an artist's weapon and, with due respect, Miss Borrodaile wasn't an artist. Ben had shaken his head again. Well, there it was. Miss Borrodaile must choose. And if she took the picklock, practise, practise, practise.

She'd chosen the picklock and she'd practised, practised, practised. Ben hadn't been easy with her, and that she had appreciated. Ben was a perfectionist and he'd never been wholly satisfied; he'd seemed to have a thousand locks and all of them she'd broken. Sometimes they'd gone at once, sometimes she'd sweated. Ben had had an old man's patience, a craftsman's passion to explain his craft. Presently Rachel hadn't been quite incompetent, and later Ben had grunted. From Ben that was a compliment. He'd never been wholly satisfied but he'd let her take the picklock.

Now she took it from her bag. Her gloves weren't on yet— Ben had been emphatic about that—and she held the picklock precisely. It was a metal cylinder, perhaps eight inches long and two across. At one end was a key blank, at the other a locking wheel. Around the cylinder were tiny thumb slides, sixty perhaps, each group controlling a stage of the blank. Inside was artistry, a master's pride.

Rachel slipped in the key blank, feeling down the first line of slides. . . . One—no; two—no; three and the faintest click. She turned the wheel once, locking the little lug against the tumbler, moving her fingers to the second row. It was the eighth before it bit and, on the third row, five.

She had moved to the next when she heard the car. It was coming along the street beyond, and it seemed to be decelerating. If it came into the cul-de-sac. . . .

She shrank against the door.

The car turned half way in, its headlights sweeping the houses opposite. Incredibly it hesitated, stopped. The driver seemed uncertain. Rachel could hear her breathing and it was very much too fast. Ten seconds of indecision, agony. . . .

A bottom gear rasped angrily, an engine began to rev again. Rachel could hear its note fade irritably. She was leaning against the door still, fighting to collect herself.

Presently she returned to the picklock. . . . Feel, slide and lock again. Turn delicately, try. Nothing—not yet. Feel, slide and lock. Try. . . . Ah. . . .

She stepped into the vestibule, shutting the door behind her, leaving the lock on the catch. The picklock was in her bag again, and she took from it her gloves. She was calm for the worst was over. Latta might wake, of course; Latta might interrupt her. In which case she'd fail. But she wouldn't be caught. The door was on the catch and. . . .

And there seemed to be a dreadful smell of gas. She stood in the vestibule sniffing. Yes, there was a gas leak somewhere.

She opened the inner door, and at once she was back in the vestibule, its door shut behind her. She choked, but silently, opening the street door an inch, breathing through the crack. God, the room was a gasometer. That sort of concentration would be lethal. If Hugh Latta were inside there. . . .

She forced herself to think. If Hugh Latta were alive then she must help him. That was a plain human duty: there wasn't an escape from it. But if she rescued him she, Rachel Borrodaile. . . .

Rachel Borrodaile would shortly be explaining herself, explaining the inexplicable. First to the police, later and worse, Charles Russell.

She shrugged with a hint of anger. She'd have to go and look.

She went about it collectedly, checking her gloves, her torch. One sally was essential, two if he were living. The first would tell her that and, if he were, the rest would finish her. She'd have to open everything—windows and all the doors. And she couldn't just leave him. He'd need artificial respiration, lights and a doctor, police.

Rachel found herself disliking the police. She wondered how long she could hold her breath. There were Japanese pearl divers who were supposed to go for minutes, but she wasn't a pearl diver. She decided it was worth a test, drawing a deep breath at the crack of the front door, turning her torch against her wristwatch. It was fifty-seven seconds before she had to breathe again, and that had been doing nothing, standing immobile. She wondered what was par.

When she was ready she filled her lungs again, stepping into the sitting-room. She shut the door behind her. She might need the vestibule again since at least she could live in it.

The torchbeam caught Latta at once, face downwards on the hearthrug. Half of her noticed that it was rather a nice Niris; the other half felt his pulse.

There wasn't a flutter.

Rachel went back into the vestibule. She'd seen enough death to have an instinct for its presence, and Dr. Hugh Latta was well past doctors. She didn't hesitate; she knew.

In the vestibule she checked again methodically. . . . The torch, the picklock, both her gloves. There'd be no finger-prints.

Rachel released the catch, shutting the front door behind her, peeling her gloves at last. She walked to the parked car, breathing in greedy gulps.

The cold dawn air was heaven.

10

COLONEL CHARLES RUSSELL was reading a second police report about Hugh Latta. Like the first it was factual, a model of objectivity. Dr. Latta's housekeeper had found him dead in a roomful of gas and had at once called the police. The gas for the stove had been on full blast, but naturally it hadn't been alight. Dr. Latta had had a large contusion on his forehead; he had apparently fallen against the fire whilst trying to light it. It was known that Dr. Latta occasionally drank—not regularly but sometimes he took more than was wholly wise—and there had been evidence that that evening he had been doing some drinking. He had turned on the gas, reached up for a match—they were still on the chimneypiece—fallen and lost consciousness. The gas had done the rest.

Or, Russell thought, a man could have rung the bell; slugged Latta as he opened; carried him to the hearthrug; turned on the gas; and left. Russell frowned. The verdict of the coroner's jury would be accidental death. He hadn't a shred of evidence to set against it, only a motive, and his relations with the police were much too good to risk by going to them with some story which at bottom would be that A—personally unidentified—had a motive to murder B, when the solid factual evidence was that B had been a victim of accident.

Nevertheless police work was one thing, the Security Executive another; the Security Executive was permitted to suppose things: indeed it was employed to. Russell reviewed the guesses. . . . These people—he flinched still from gang—these Cypriots had motive to kill Latta. Latta's reputation had been one of a certain venality, and Russell was too experienced to imagine that if he had been able to discover that fact himself nobody else could. And it wouldn't suit these people to have Mecron declared innocuous. So, guessing again, they'd had a man look at Latta's papers, and what he had reported hadn't suited them. It was a pity the Executive hadn't had sight of them first, but it wouldn't have saved Latta if it had. Latta had had it coming.

. . . Hm. Very neat, but it was unsupported. Or rather it stood on the hypothesis that Mecron could be big business to a considerable organization. But that, alas, wasn't mere hypothesis. Mecron *could* be important. Anybody planning to peddle it as a narcotic, and to quite new buyers, wouldn't want it put back in the shops again. That would kill business at once.

Kill. Russell rose quickly, striding his room. If these Cypriots had killed Latta they were indeed considerable. Rachel Borrodaile had said they were, and Miss Borrodaile was reliable with her facts. Russell tried to think as they would. Orthodox narcotics weren't a major problem in Britain. The system was incredible but incredibly it worked. There were countries where you risked a serious sentence for being an addict, or at least for not reporting it. You could be compulsorily treated—outlawed. But here all that happened was that you went to your doctor, and your doctor, grumbling, making Hippocratic noises, gave you the minimum to keep you normal. That wasn't quite true in detail but it was a valid generalization. Foreign police raised their eyebrows; foreign police were incredulous. But somehow it seemed to work. Of course there were leaks, but they were marginal. Narcotics weren't big business since the margin wasn't big enough. But a brand new drug to a brand new sort of addict could be very tempting bait.

Russell sat down again. If he were these Cypriots he'd be doing just as they seemed to be; he'd be disposing of anybody who threatened the future, and he'd be trying to lay his hands on enough Mecron to keep the market open.

Until he could play it big—import the filth in bulk. And that reminded him. He must find out how much delay Hugh Latta's death would involve. Presumably it wouldn't be serious; presumably a scientific inquiry didn't have to start again from scratch because the man who had been going to sign the final report had been—well, had met with an accident. With Latta dead Mecron would be declared a dangerous drug, and when it was the orthodox machinery could take over. Putting it on prescription at the least, watching it. . . . And the sooner the better.

When it wouldn't be Russell's problem.

Nevertheless he rose again uneasily. It looked all right, but this wouldn't be the first time this Mecron affair had looked all right, then flared unexpectedly. He checked it mentally. . . . Latta was dead, so if Mecron were dangerous it would honestly be found so. After that this gang would be up against an efficient and tried machine, this gang. . . .

Russell laughed suddenly, for suddenly he knew what worried him. . . . This gang! He'd used the term unthinkingly, and unconsciously it had helped him. It was a word taboo in the Executive, but the taboo wasn't a question of too delicate sensibilities: on the contrary reason supported it, for a gang was an abstraction and abstractions didn't work. Abstractions didn't peddle drugs, nor steal them. Men did these things, dangerous and determined men, and any body of determined men had one thing in common. They always owned a leader and in this case he wasn't known.

Russell looked at the clock. In an hour and a half he was going to a theatre. He was a considerable theatregoer; he took one Sunday newspaper solely to read its theatrical critic. Then he made a list of his recommendations and carefully avoided them. But he still found plenty to go to.

Now he forgot his theatre, for he was engaged in something more fascinating than the play of any stranger; he was seeing Mecron for himself as drama, good commercial theatre of the sort he enjoyed. He took a sheet of thick cream foolscap, writing on it firmly *Dramatis Personae*. This struck him as old-fashioned and he crossed it out. He wrote *CAST* instead and lit a pipe, settling to think deliciously.

. . . You didn't start with the protagonist. Russell didn't know why, but competent playwrights didn't. They started

92

with a couple of minor parts, people who introduced the principals, pushed the first act along. In one sort of play it had been butler and parlourmaid, but today that was very old hat. Russell rather regretted the butler and parlourmaid, for theatrically they hadn't been less effective than a woman scrubbing frying pans or, in the really advanced school, a defecating drunk. Still, they wouldn't do here. This wasn't social comedy, but nor was it South-West Three. Russell wrote confidently:

Ronald Davis	*A biochemist*
Peter Davis	*His brother, a civil servant*
Dr. Hugh Latta	*A venal scientist*

That would do nicely. The three of them ran it along a bit, carried you to the first crisis. . . . Whose crisis? Why, Henry Leggatt's, naturally.

Henry Leggatt	*Parliamentary Secretary to the Ministry of Social Welfare*

Good—really excellent. One could do things with Henry Leggatt. He was an obvious protagonist but not too painfully a hero. Rather to the contrary. Poor chap he was in a spot, and that was a very good start. He was a Minister whose firm —ex-firm to be accurate—was making a drug which they seemed to be still confident was safe but which plenty of other people, politicians and newspapers included, were very far from sure about. And his wife, if you listened at parties, was common gossip-fodder.

Charles Russell took his pen again. Of course, that was another thing—the love interest. Henry Leggatt was married unhappily; he'd married soon after the war, a slip of a girl she'd been, and one didn't need to be more than reasonably observant to realize that the marriage had surprised Miss Borrodaile. He needn't put it higher than surprised. Not for an act or two.

Rachel Borrodaile   *An officer of the Security Executive*

. . . Yes, pretty good still. If he wasn't damned careful he'd be writing the thing in detail, hawking it round the agents. But he knew there was something missing: he had his hero but he didn't have his villain. Indeed the villain's absence had started his train of thought, for the villain was Miss Borrodaile's gang, and gangs were impersonal. This one was dangerous; it was known to the police and well; it could have killed Dr. Latta. But it was no sort of human character.

Russell wrote tentatively:

Mr. Robert Seneschal   Minister of Social Welfare

but shook his head at once. Seneschal was one of the most dislikeable men he knew but that didn't make him an antagonist. He'd come in again somewhere, he was much too unpleasant to waste, but he wasn't the villain. Inescapably the villain was a gang, and clearly a gang wouldn't do. So flop went a promising story. Charles Russell, amateur playwright, was a little disappointed, but Colonel Charles Russell of the Security Executive was not. He had experience to back his hunch. A gang wouldn't do but a gang was people, and from any group of people someone would always emerge. And with any sort of luck he'd be wholly appropriate, Henry Leggatt's opposite, social and flash and smooth. And dangerous, naturally.

Charles Russell smiled happily. He'd be in the West End yet, in lights above the portico. That was something he'd insist on.

In the little house in Albert Street a bald man was talking quietly. 'Quite a clean job, I think. No fuss and no traces.'

'Good,' Asher said.

'But the rest of it isn't.'

'Why not?'

'We're running very short of it—the stuff.'

'But why? What's the latest from Rikky?'

'We can't rely on Rikky, or not yet. He's doing his best, but there's something about this Mecron. You get the things together, all according to the formula, and mix them. Then you try it out since you're not a fool and . . . and nothing. It simply doesn't bite.' There was a very unEnglish shrug. 'I tell you there's something *about* this stuff. Maybe these Hassertons don't know it themselves. Rikky's got a nice little laboratory bang in the middle of a Turkish village where nobody would look for one, and Rikky's a damned good chemist. He's tried several times and it simply doesn't work. It sends you to sleep all right, but so do lots of other things. You even wake feeling good. But you don't want the stuff again, you can take it or leave it. You're not on the hook. There isn't one.'

'Better put it back again.'

'You don't think that Rikky's not trying. He'll get it in time and then we're clear away. But it's the time that bothers us.'

'I can see.'

'Two gross of Mecron we stole—a nothing. Barely enough for the people already hooked, nothing to go fishing with. And people on the hook can often be very awkward when you can't meet their needs.' This time there was a pause, well-timed. 'Sometimes they get desperate; sometimes they even talk.'

'They better hadn't.'

'Easy to say.' The bald man wasn't frightened of Dick Asher; he respected his brains, accepting his leadership, but he wasn't a stooge. 'Easy to make noises, but suppose someone did. At exactly the wrong time for us. Sooner or later the heat will go slap on Mecron. We've always known that for it's part of the game. But no heat's worth fighting for a handful of notes across some sleazy café table. We're not that sort of business.' The bald man showed superlative white teeth; he said in resonant English: 'So give us the tools and—'

'How much do you want?'

'Enough to keep going until Rikky makes it click.'

'All right,' Asher said, 'I'll get you some more.'

11

PATRICIA LEGGATT DIDN'T often get up in time to
breakfast with her husband. He made his own coffee and
hers, gulping a roll before rushing to the ministry. But this
morning was Saturday, and they were eating together late.
Patricia was in a dressing-gown, but otherwise her toilet was
complete. She always took trouble with her appearance—even
for her husband, he thought unhappily—but apart from her
appearance she wasn't troubling at all. She was reading *The
Gong*, not eating but smoking a cigarette. He mightn't have
been there.

He looked about the room, noticing the new curtains,
wondering how they had been paid for or, if they hadn't,
how he could. It had been different when he'd been in Hassertons: then he could have afforded them comfortably. As it
was he was perpetually pinched. Patricia wasn't good with
money. Their account was a joint one and she wasn't always
wise with it. Once or twice she had landed him, for Patricia
was rich. He corrected himself. His wife wasn't rich, or not
in the sense of owning money, but she was accustomed to
money around her. The distinction was important to ordinary
people like himself or bankers, but Patricia seemed never to
have grasped it.

Henry Leggatt was on edge for he had passed a miserable
week, one made more wretched by the corrosive knowledge
that he ought to take some action. But he was a careful man,
the inferences pointed all ways, and he didn't like moving
without solid facts. He didn't want a showdown with Patricia
—he told himself glumly that he couldn't afford one—but if
it did come to that his instinct was for a single issue, something simple to stick on. But now, mentally stale and frus-
trated, he wasn't so sure he had it. She was clever at answers

—good woman's answers. He was fifteen years older, a busy, too-busy man. It couldn't be very amusing being the wife of an overworked junior Minister. Naturally she'd seek company.

He shook his head. It wouldn't do, all this was quite unreal. It was playing with fine ideas, not facing a situation. He was putting her own arguments, perhaps too well, but Dick Asher was fact, not argument. He'd have to tackle her, he'd have to be firm, and he wasn't very good at being firm, or not with Patricia. His sister had never liked her, and once she'd been brutally frank; she'd told him he was afraid of her. He'd laughed but he'd flushed. Not just uncertain—plenty of husbands were that—but tangled in something which psychiatrists had very ugly words for. If that were true Patricia had him cold, and it wasn't a good thing for a woman to have you cold.

But that was an odious thought, disloyal without reason. A man who could think like that deserved. . . .

He didn't know what he deserved. He knew what he wanted and he wasn't getting it.

And it didn't make it easier that she'd set her heart on Christmas at Cortina. Cortina wasn't his own idea of Christmas, but Patricia was determined. And perhaps at Cortina, together. . . .

He took from his pocket a letter four days old. It was one from his bank, polite, he thought ironically, as a letter to a Member of Parliament should be. But unmistakably firm. He was four hundred pounds overdrawn and he'd been so for more than six months. There was nothing behind it, the loan was quite uncovered. The manager regretted, but Head Office. . . .

It was a formula he'd seen before.

Henry finished his coffee, rising heavily. 'I must be off.'

'On Saturday? Why don't you take it easy?' She looked at him, not personally engaged but with a nurse's disinterested compassion. 'You don't look very well.'

'I'm all right. And I've one or two things to do.'

'I think you'd be better resting.' She picked up *The Gong* again, asking casually from behind it: 'What things? Won't they wait?'

'I must go to the bank.'

'So soon again? You went on Monday. I hadn't expected . . . .'

She had spoken sharply, and he looked up quickly, curious. *The Gong* was down, her head erect. Her face told him nothing, but her back had straightened from its accustomed loll. 'Do you have to go today? It's Saturday. Why don't you rest?'

'I'm afraid we're in the red again.'

She moved her shoulders with a hint of resignation. He was puzzled but put it aside. At least she was considering him, and for that he was grateful.

A little too grateful, he told himself, a trifle too thankful for nothing.

He walked to his bank, disturbed by discovering that a mile was much more tiring than it should have been. He was outrageously out of condition; he must do something about it and soon. He went into the bank, asking for his statement, knowing at once from the clerk's manner that something unusual had happened. Bank clerks had special manners when you asked for your statement across the counter, and Henry had wondered whether they acquired them naturally or whether they were taught at one of the extravagant staff-training schools which joint stock banks maintained in what had once been houses. In either case the manner was instantly recognizable. If you were up the clerk would be congratulatory—wordlessly and discreetly, but unmistakably an associate in good fortune no doubt deserved. But if you were down he wouldn't imply discredit. Most certainly not. He would be the family physician who knew you were dying slowly but had decided he mustn't mention it.

Henry looked at his statement. They were a hundred to the good.

He looked at the figure in detail. There was a credit entry

for five hundred pounds. Three days ago, he saw. He couldn't account for it.

He called the clerk, pointing. 'Can you tell me where this came from?'

'I'll look it up, sir.'

The clerk went away, returning with a white pay-in slip. In his best associate manner he said smoothly: 'It was paid in at this branch, sir. Across the counter. By a Mr. Richard Asher. I remember it myself. I didn't know the payer, but Mrs. Leggatt was with him.'

Henry knew what he must do. He knew where Dick Asher banked, for he had once cashed a tenner for him. He hadn't much liked doing it, but he needn't have worried. The cheque had been met without question, and Henry remembered the bank since it hadn't been a common one. It had been painstakingly antiquated, a survival which he had heard of but wouldn't have dreamt of using. His money wasn't big enough.

'Give me a pink slip, please.'

He made out the slip to credit of Mr. Richard Asher at Arbuthnots in Pall Mall, beginning on a cheque for five hundred pounds. When he had written half of it he stopped; he looked again at his statement. He had a hundred in hand and he was writing a cheque for five. That would be four hundred down again. The bank wouldn't bounce his cheque, but he was an overdrawn customer, long overdrawn, and the manager would be curious. . . . Here was a Member of Parliament, four hundred pounds to the bad and under pressure to square his account. So five hundred pounds goes in on one day, not a pay day at that, and, three days later, out it all goes again. Odd—very odd. The manager would want his money still; he might start to look at details, clearings and slips. . . . Five hundred pounds from a Mr. Richard Asher. He wouldn't know Dick Asher but he'd know about Arbuthnots; he'd be impressed by Arbuthnots. . . . Five hundred pounds from a Mr. Richard Asher and, impossibly, five hundred pounds straight back to this Mr. Asher.

Well, well, well. A Member of Parliament at that. Take

a letter, Miss Smith. . . . To Henry Leggatt, Esquire,
M.P. Dear Mr. Leggatt. With reference to my letter of
last week, comma, I am afraid my Head Office is again
insisting. . . .

Henry Leggatt destroyed the pink slip slowly, then, even
more deliberately, his unsigned cheque. In any case that
wouldn't be good discharge: this wasn't something to be
settled by some furious gesture of honour. Patricia had
accepted five hundred pounds of another man's money. He'd
try and think later why she hadn't just taken cash. It was
odd—she wasn't brazen. And bringing Dick Asher along
with her! But none of that was essential. The essential was
that she'd accepted five hundred pounds of another man's
money. Four hundred rather, for she'd left him, contemptu-
ously, a hundred pounds.

. . . And that had been his marriage. Sometime he'd pick
the pieces up. Perhaps.

He doubted it.

Henry waited until the evening before tackling Patricia.
He wasn't a man who laughed a lot, but nor was he insensitive
to irony, and the situation struck him as ironical. For in a way
he had been looking forward to this evening. They didn't eat
many domestic dinners, one of them was nearly always
out, but when they did he enjoyed them. Patricia didn't
cook, but the daily woman did, and well; she would leave
something in the oven, something good. Henry helped
to serve it, and he opened a bottle of claret. And afterwards, over the fire, Patricia relaxing, soaking the heat up
sensuously. . . .

Irony shrank suddenly in bitter fact. It wouldn't be one of
those evenings. Anyway, they'd been growing fewer.

In the event he didn't wait for dinner. He saw that she
had had three drinks, and after three drinks Patricia grew
sleepy. He took one himself and a deliberate breath.

'I went to the bank today.'

'I know.' She was perfectly collected.

'We were four hundred down and now we're not. You'd been to the bank with Dick Asher. He gave you five hundred and you took it.'

'But he didn't.'

He said, conscious it sounded pompous: 'The facts are there.'

She laughed and it threw him off-stride. The laugh hadn't been forced, nor even malicious. Patricia was genuinely amused. 'If you're thinking I've been taking money from a man, forget it. I took nothing we weren't owed.'

'I don't think I understand.'

'I sold Dick something for five hundred pounds.'

'We've nothing worth five hundred.'

'I sold him that box of Mecron.' Her voice hadn't changed.

'Christ,' he said finally. 'God in heaven.'

'Why—what's the fuss?'

'Don't you read the newspapers?'

'I read *The Gong*, if you call that a newspaper.'

'If you read *The Gong* you must know there's been trouble about Mecron. And if you took an ordinary newspaper you'd know that there's been trouble in the House.'

She said calmly: 'Who's going to know? Who'll ever find out? We were four hundred down and we hadn't a hope of clearing it. Now we're a hundred up. We can go to Cortina.'

'We're much more likely to go to gaol.'

'Oh Henry. . . .'

He saw at once that he had blundered. Exaggeration wasn't safe with Patricia Leggatt, unthinking hyperbole played up to her. She had a literal mind and used it.

She was using it now, taking an immediate advantage. 'Why don't you have a bath? We'll talk about it later, though it's done.'

He decided the advice was sound. For a moment she'd wrong-footed him, magically the initiative was hers. Magically and he resented it.

He was dressing again when the telephone rang, and he walked into the living-room in vest and trousers. There had been a time when Henry Leggatt had looked well in vest and trousers, but now he was carrying that fatal extra stone. Not that he was considering a more than nascent belly; he was watching his wife. She had been listless but now she was vividly alive .again. As he came in bare-footed he heard her say gaily: 'Of course I'll come, and bless you for asking me. You've saved my life.' She put down the telephone, turning to him quickly. 'I shan't be eating in tonight.'

'You can't do that.'

'Why not?'

'We made a date.'

'Then we'll make one tomorrow instead.'

'You're going to the country tomorrow.'

For an instant she was embarrassed. 'I'm sorry—I'd for-gotten.' But she recovered at once. 'All right, we'll call it Monday. We'll make a private date for Monday.'

Henry ignored her. He began to talk quickly, almost by reflex, his voice rising sharply in cadences he didn't recognize. . . . That Mecron that hadn't been hers to dispose of. That Asher man. Five hundred pounds. . . . He was doing it the worst way possible; he did not care. Something more power-ful than reason gripped him, the resentments of years, con-sciously suppressed but darkly breeding, a nagging knowledge of an inferiority which he had never admitted since he had neved dared acknowledge its existence. Patricia Leggatt— Patricia Egham. Poor fool, he'd desired her and desired her still. He heard a high tense voice say stupidly: 'I wonder you married me.'

'I told you at the time. I liked you.'

For a moment her cool voice calmed him. It was the truth. At least she was honest. She'd never said she loved him.

Patricia was an Egham, a cadet, a collateral Egham. She had her own damned sense of honour.

She began to move away, into the bedroom they no longer shared, perfectly collected still. That broke him finally. She hadn't the right to be calm, no sort of right at all. It was an arrogance, intolerable. He said savagely: 'Who are you going out with?'

'Must you know that?'

'Who are you going out with?'

'Dick Asher,' she said.

He began to curse brutally, calling her names he knew were past forgiving. Her expression changed slightly but she didn't protest. She stood lightly, beautifully balanced, watching him impersonally, like a servant, he thought helplessly, some suddenly crazed servant. He hadn't touched her—couldn't. When he drew breath she said: 'And if I did have a lover?'

It hit him as once a shell blast had. He hadn't been hurt, but instantly he'd been extremely sober. He'd had a ration rum or two but he'd picked himself up stone sober. He picked himself up now, very sober indeed. . . . 'And if I did have a lover?' That was what she'd said. 'If I did have a lover. . . .'

He didn't know the answer, and come to think of it there wasn't one. Violence—knock her about a bit? A minute ago and he might have done it, but now he was emotionally cold. Unexpectedly he shivered and he almost smiled. So his body was cold too, his middle-aged body. He was a middle-aged man in vest and trousers, a middle-aged man with more than the beginnings of a belly; he was facing a wife much younger, and the wife had admitted—well, not exactly admitted. . . .

Not that the distinction mattered. He hadn't an answer anyway.

He turned on his heel, walking to his dressing-room unsteadily.

She'd beaten him again.

He took another bath for he was trembling. He heard her changing in the bedroom, the front door click behind her. He remembered there was something he hadn't asked her—she hadn't let him. She'd sold Dick Asher a carton of Mecron but she hadn't taken cash, and Dick Asher was stiff with cash. He was the sort of man who carried it in wads. She'd dragged him to the bank instead. . . .

He climbed from the bath clumsily. He was emotionally exhausted, mentally and physically all in. He found a bottle of whisky and began to drink deliberately.

She'd taken his cheque, she'd taken him to the bank. . . . That didn't matter now.

12

THE RESTAURANT TO which Henry Leggatt took Rachel
next evening was one of perhaps half a dozen which she could
have guessed he would choose. It was solid without being
tiresomely grand, and the service, though a little too friendly
for some tastes, was at least unEnglish and therefore willing.
Being a waiter wasn't something which the waiters resented:
on the contrary it was a profession and a perfectly respectable
one. In the bar they drank two large gins, or rather Henry
did. He had remembered that Rachel loathed short drinks,
and Rachel had been flattered. It was clear, she decided, that
he hadn't forgotten everything—not quite everything. The
evening was off to an excellent start.

At table Henry ordered quickly. He wasn't imaginative,
but it wasn't an imaginative restaurant. Rachel watched him
eat, thinking that he didn't know how to. He was a long way
from being greedy, but for a man noticeably overweight he
was surprisingly ignorant. He ate bread and a good deal of
fried potato; he seemed to like fat and everything he shouldn't.
Rachel caught herself reflecting that later, when they'd picked
the threads up, she might risk the discreetest hint.

The thought annoyed her. . . . Later, when they'd picked
the threads up. . . . But they might never do so. Henry
had asked her to dinner because she worked in the Security
Executive. The evening was a business evening, and as that
it might end. She must watch herself; she wasn't a girl.

But it wasn't the Security Executive that Henry began to
talk about. As the wine warmed him he began to speak of
politics. Rachel listened intently. Shop fascinated her, for she
knew that most men were interesting only when they were
talking it. As long as one hadn't heard it all that fatal time
too often. And behind the technicalities were a man's own

view of them, his thoughts and his unconscious judgements. No man could wholly hide them and not all tried. And that was personality, a woman's business.

Rachel went on listening, saying little beyond an occasional prompt. She remembered that she had once thought of him as a gentleman in waiting, a man through some doors but not the one that mattered, never in Henry's party, waiting, waiting for the entry which he hadn't a hope of. She knew now she'd been right. She remembered his background too, the country vicarage and minor public school, then business from the dustiest of bottoms. He'd been twenty-two when war broke out, and off he'd gone to it. Then gallant and completely useful service, but not the sort which helped with Henry's party, not with the right people. Afterwards there'd been business again and a deserved success. Finally politics. . . . Politics! He was Parliamentary Secretary to the Ministry of Welfare, and there he'd stick. Henry hadn't the right smell; Henry hadn't an earthly.

She wondered again whether he had sensed the trap. Apparently not still, though he mightn't be far from it. Rachel listened with more than ears, her sensibilities at concert pitch. No, he mightn't be far from final disillusionment. Robert Seneschal, for instance: Henry spoke of Seneschal as Minister, a kind of boss, never as colleague. Seneschal was a different sort of animal, though Henry hadn't faced it yet. In Henry's subconscious Seneschal was 'they' still. Rachel suppressed a shrug, guessing at what would happen when finally he brought himself to 'we'.

Presently he came round to the Executive. He had drunk a good deal of wine besides the gin, and the drink had relaxed him. For the second time Rachel mistrusted it. Alcohol was the best of servants, but a man shouldn't need so much of it to talk just comfortably. Nevertheless she was grateful to the wine which Henry had put below a belt which she couldn't help observing. For he was coming to business.

He was asking: 'So you like the Security Executive?'

'I like it well enough.'

'It does a useful job.'

'We flatter ourselves that sometimes. . . .' Rachel grimaced. 'There's a mass of routine and it isn't always pleasant. But sometimes we can help people.

'I was wondering if that went for me.'

? . . Here it comes.

'We could try.'

'It's pretty—well, it's pretty personal.'

'It always is.'

'Not official, I mean.'

'Of course.'

Henry drank some wine, and Rachel asked politely: 'Can I have some cheese, please?' Cheese would be just as well. She didn't want him fuddled; she wanted his story.

'I'll have some too.' Henry began on Stilton, saying between mouthfuls: 'Have you heard of Mecron?'

'I certainly have. *The Gong* got hold of it and smeared it. Then there was a row in Parliament.'

'It smeared me too.'

'I know. I read the papers and Hansard as well when. . . .'

She left it unfinished. She had been going to say: 'when there's anything that interests us,' but that would have been untimely. She didn't want to scare him.

'Then you'll know that Mecron is made by Hassertons, and Hassertons is my firm, or was.'

She nodded, waiting.

'Something may have gone wrong with it. Hassertons must think otherwise—they're not the sort of people to deal in suspect drugs—and there's the fact that they didn't drop it quietly when they could have. By now there's been enough fuss about the thing to force an inquiry about it. That Dr. Latta of the Templeton was doing it and the Templeton still is. We're waiting for the result, and you can be sure Hassertons are working on it themselves. Meanwhile they're distributing no more.'

'Most of that came out in Parliament.'

'Not all of it,' he said.

'That wouldn't be unusual.'

He managed a smile though she could see he was deadly

108

serious. 'No. But in this case it wasn't the Mother of Parliaments being taken for her accustomed ride.'

'Who was it then?'

'I—I wish I knew. It might be me.'

'Better spill it,' she said.

He began to do so, haltingly, stumbling, only his eyes steadily on her face. 'The important part to me is that Hassertons agreed to put out no more Mecron till the Templeton had done the test. And I had some Mecron with me, quite a lot as it happened—two gross of tubes. The sales manager sent me a carton thinking, I dare say, that I could tout it, push it along a bit. I didn't, of course. In fact I nearly forgot it. And now—now I'm afraid I've lost it.'

'Lost it?'

'Actually rather worse.'

'Why worse?'

Under the table her hands were clenched.

'Patricia took it without my knowledge. Then she sold the carton. All of it. For five hundred pounds.'

Rachel said involuntarily: 'Five hundred pounds.' Her face was white.

'Then you know something too?' Henry was very tense. And not a fool, she thought.

'Never mind about me. Your *wife* took it? *Sold* it?'

'We were dreadfully hard up.'

'That doesn't alter it. . . . Your wife sold your Mecron?'

He nodded miserably.

'To whom?'

'To a man called Dick Asher.'

But Rachel was shaking her head. 'I've never heard of him.' It happened to be true. 'Who is he?'

'He's a Cypriot.'

'A Cypriot!' Rachel was almost standing. 'Did you say a Cypriot?'

'Yes. Does it matter?'

'It matters like hell.' She recovered herself slowly but thinking fast; at last she said: 'I'll have to trust you as you've trusted me. We *do* know something about Mecron that probably you don't. I'm not saying now that it's a habit-forming drug, but plenty of people seem to want it remarkably badly. They'll pay the earth for it, and when there's that sort of demand then somebody steps in to fill it. In drugs it's the black market. Somehow the black market has got hold of Mecron, and the black market in this case is the Cypriots.'

Her heart turned over as she watched his face. But it didn't fall to pieces. She saw him raise his wine glass, finally put it down again. His jaw tightened suddenly.

'I see.'

'I'm glad I don't have to hammer it.'

'No, you don't have to rub it in. I see—I see, all right.' His voice was grim.

But Rachel was professional again; she asked professionally: 'You say there was a sale. But is there any proof of it?'

'Patricia took a cheque. She paid it in.'

'To *her* account?'

'To ours. We've a joint one.' Henry had contrived a smile and Rachel respected it. 'Not that the technicalities would save me. She's my wife and I'm a Minister. That's what's going to sink me.'

'It looks rather like it.'

There was an uncomfortable silence which Henry broke; he said, more than a little hesitant: 'Rachel, can you help me?'

'I can try.' She was thinking that she could try, but she was too experienced to underestimate extortion. The easy line with blackmail was to tell the person blackmailed to go straight to the police. When the blackmailer lost his weapon. It was the advice the police themselves gave and often it worked admirably, but it was rule-of-thumb procedure by no means infallible, since blackmailers worked for a variety of motives. The common or garden brand, happily most of them, wanted just money, and, once you had come clean, to police or others interested, bang went their handle. That was the standard case, not a matter for the Executive at all. But this didn't look standard; there were loud overtones of politics, besides a considerable organization interested in what could be considerable business. And there was something else which Rachel couldn't quite put her finger on. Her instinct was that it was personal. She shivered, knowing that the blackmailer for malice would ignore the formal countermoves. It wouldn't be easy to frighten him since his motives weren't purely commercial. At a crisis it wouldn't move him that he destroyed himself too. And with the wife in it as well. . . .

Rachel Borrodaile had heard things—gossip but too much of it. She couldn't offer Henry easy comfort—dare not. For Henry it was going to get a whole lot worse before it could get better.

If it ever did get better.

As matter-of-fact as she could make herself she asked: 'Tell me about this Asher.'

'There isn't a great deal to tell. I don't really know him. He seems to have plenty of money and no job that I know of. He amuses Patricia. He's her friend, not mine.'

'A close one?'

'Very.'

He had answered too quickly. She could see that he had flushed but she did not release his eyes. She was more than half in love again, but for the moment she was an officer of the Executive.

'Well?'

'I . . . I. . . .' He hesitated, but returning her calm inspection. She wasn't an individual. She wasn't because she didn't dare to be, though he wasn't to know that. She was an official, indifferent as a nameless grave, and maybe she could help him.

'I . . . we. . . .'

It all came tumbling out, slowly at first, then quickening in sudden rushes. Sometimes he wouldn't face an actual word. Then a wry smile, a shrug, hands spread. . . . Patricia Egham. The marriage that now wasn't. It hadn't been her fault perhaps. She'd come from another world, one privileged, protected, gay, and back to it she'd drifted. Not that he'd married her to pass a gate he hadn't known existed. She'd influence no doubt, the connection that any Egham brought into the world by birth, even the least of them. But he hadn't sought that. It might have been better if he had, for then she'd have been an asset like another, something to watch and cultivate. Instead he'd worked too hard. In any case she'd never loved him. That he had known, accepting it. He'd fallen for her helplessly, taking her terms, hardly believing his good fortune. He'd worked and worked; he'd had to justify. And now, and now. . . . Dick Asher and his wife. Dick Asher and this Mecron. A cheque for five hundred. . . .

His voice died unhappily, a sudden energy spent suddenly. Rachel saw that he had finished. There were things that he hadn't said, things that he never would. Henry Leggatt had finished but Rachel could guess them.

She said carefully: 'About this cheque. He sent it to her, of course. And when did you find out?'

'When I went to my bank yesterday.'

'She'd paid it in? That's what you said, I think.'

For a second he hesitated again. 'Not exactly.'

'I don't think I follow.'

'She didn't pay it in. Dick Asher did.'

'But she knew?'

'She knew all right.'

'You're sure?'

'I'm certain.'

'I've got to ask it. How?'

He dropped his eyes, saying to the tablecloth: 'They went to the bank together. Both of them. The clerk remembers it.'

When he looked up again Rachel was on her feet. A waiter was holding her fur. Henry said sickly: 'I'm afraid I've offended you.'

She couldn't help smiling. 'You've not offended me. I've work to do, that's all. Get me a taxi, please.'

'Where to?'

'To the Security Executive.'

'The Executive?' he repeated. It sounded stupid and he realized it.

'That's where I work. Not that I'm making promises. It's serious.'

'It's serious for me.'

'And me as well. I've bought a piece of this.' She managed a laugh. 'For what that's worth to you.'

It was very quiet in the Security Executive. Rachel went to her room, ringing the night bell, and the duty officer answered it.

'Do we know anything about a Richard Asher?'

'I've never heard of him myself. Not that that means a lot. What's he been doing? What are his contacts?'

'His contact as far as we're concerned is Henry Leggatt of the Ministry of Welfare. His business is illicit drugs and blackmail. He's a Cypriot who lives here.'

'I'll chase it up at once.'

Ten minutes later the duty officer came back again. 'I'm afraid we've nothing on him.'

'Then send across the road and ask what they know. It's late but they'll play. My compliments, of course.'

'I'll go myself.'

Rachel didn't have to wait long. She plunged into what was evidently a considerable dossier. Richard Asher. . . . It was his real name and a remarkable story. His father had been a British soldier who had settled in Cyprus, marrying a woman of the island. In retirement he had made a good deal of money, and Dick Asher had been educated in England. But though his English was perfect he had never assimilated. Nor, it seemed, tried to. When his parents had died he had inherited a substantial fortune, but none of the English ways of spending one had attracted him. He had stayed as he had been born—a Mediterranean, a Greek. And by instinct a criminal, since it couldn't be necessity which drove him. He lived very well and in circles considered smart. These were his contacts and mostly his victims. And it was clear he despised them. He had kept aloof from politics, orthodox politics and their dubious periphery which was especially the Executive's business. The Executive didn't know him since it didn't need to.

But colleagues did, and well. He was known to the police as an accomplished criminal. Thrice they had nearly nailed him and thrice they hadn't. One case in particular rankled. They had thought that at last they had him, the Public Prosecutor's office had sweated a lawyer's surrogate for blood, but finally. . . .

Finally Dick Asher was still free. And operating. He operated in women and, when he could get them, drugs. And in extortion, naturally. The three went together in unholy marriage. Sell a man women and blackmail him later. Sell a man drugs and hook him for keeps. Bleed him white. The thing had a classic, a Greek simplicity.

Rachel began to smile, thinking that people had the oddest ideas about the Greeks. Eminent novelists went to Greece in their forties and at once lost their heads. But never their pens. They wrote of dark green olive trees sweeping down to an improbably blue sea, of impossibly white temples on romantic hills, their ageless stone glowing in a too mellow sun. Well, perhaps; perhaps not. But the people—goodness, they had got the people wrong. They saw them as innocents, as charming, simple peasants; they saw them as the conscious heirs of a tradition which they themselves had more than half imagined. . . . Dubious dons from doubtful colleges conducting the English schoolmistress who for years had grimly saved for it, the richer and much less sympathetic culture-vultures; touting them round the Isles of Greece for passage and pocket money, spouting bad Greek, pointing the sights out, the funny clothes brought out to show the tourists; falsifying.

Greeks weren't like that at all; Greeks were earth's toughest race. For centuries they'd had to be and, under the profitable shams, they were so still. Greeks could look after themselves.

Dick Asher, for instance: it was evident Dick Asher could look after himself. He was English by birth, he held a British passport, but he was Greek by choice and nature. Greek in his ruthlessness, his contempt for convention. He'd see in Henry Leggatt most things he detested.

And he was tangled with his wife. Henry hadn't put it

114

in terms—Henry was very English—but Rachel didn't doubt it. She rose abstractedly, walking to the mirror, putting her fist behind her head, the middle two fingers folded. The first and fourth stuck out. The horns, she thought, the fine old horns. It wasn't a pretty gesture and it wasn't a pretty thing, but contempt for the wearer was mostly exaggerated, a convention and a blind one. It wasn't only the pompous who wore the ancient badge—the Napoleons, Anglican bishops and the M.C.C.; these carried the horns deservedly, they were good for a hearty laugh; but decent men could wear them too and that wasn't funny. The horns of Henry Leggatt weren't contemptible for nor was he.

Rachel sat down at her desk again, glancing at the clock, surprised that it was well past three. But she did not move, for she knew that sleep would be impossible. Henry Leggatt was in trouble and that meant she was too. She was facing that now. Henry Leggatt could be ground exceeding small and that meant he mustn't be. But it wouldn't be easy. Blackmail at least was certain, but she didn't know the brand of it. It might be straight money, but she didn't think so. Henry wasn't rich. There was a great deal more money in Mecron than Henry would ever see.

Reluctantly she acknowledged it: the next move against Henry would be a demand for more Mecron. Never mind how he was to get it—from Hassertons perhaps. Never mind the details, for Asher himself wouldn't bother with them. He wouldn't suggest, he'd demand. He'd ask for more Mecron or else.

. . . Go to the police after all? That was orthodox advice but it wouldn't save Henry. For a Minister's wife had been dealing in a suspect if not yet formally disreputable drug, and at a price which she must have known was much above its ordinary value. Moreover she'd sold it to a man the police would love to nail. There were liberal and obliging policemen at the top, and for colleagues in the Security Executive they were willing to be something more than liberal. But this wasn't a matter which you could ask them to ignore. A bland absence of action was one thing, suppression quite another, and active suppression was what it would amount to. Besides, whatever the police did, Asher himself wouldn't suppress. Go after Asher and at once he would implicate Henry.

And Patricia Leggatt—there was a *bad* one.

Which left the Security Executive: after all Henry had approached it. Rachel sighed softly. He hadn't approached the Security Executive but her. Russell was interested in Mecron—she'd never seen him so personally engaged—but tell him that Patricia Leggatt had been selling it to the black market and the Leggatts would be his enemies. Both of them. He wasn't in love with Henry Leggatt, he wasn't even friendly with him. Russell would act—oh yes, he'd act. Charles Russell hated Mecron; he'd destroy it if he could, and certainly those who fattened on it. He was privately convinced it was a dangerous drug and damn the tedious proofs. Personalities wouldn't weigh with him. He'd see it as a duty and Rachel couldn't blame him.

Which left her alone. Well, it wouldn't be the first time.

For an instant she wavered. With the Executive behind her. . . . But no, she couldn't risk it. Tell Russell the facts and Henry would be finished.

She picked up the telephone, remembering that Patricia Leggatt was in the country. She dialled Henry's number.

'Henry?'

'Rachel, aren't you in bed yet?'

'Were *you* asleep?'

He said dourly: 'I was not.'

'Then no more am I. What I wanted to say was that I left you too quickly. There were obvious things I should have told you.'

'I don't need to hear the obvious. They're going to go after me.'

'I didn't mean that. I meant the mechanics, the keeping in touch. You're to tell me at once if anything develops.' She gave him a number. 'That's reasonably secure.'

'You're an awfully good scout.'

She banged down the telephone, furious. Russell had called her a good soldier and now Henry a good scout. But she wasn't a good soldier and she wasn't a good scout. She wasn't, she wasn't, she wasn't. Blast all good soldiers, curse all scouts. She was Rachel Borrodaile, a woman.

Slowly anger faded. She was a woman, but she was one with a load of mischief. She was a senior security officer with a powerful machine behind her. But she couldn't invoke it. She was alone again indeed. She was back in the old routine.

In the room in Camden Town Dick Asher was asking easily: 'Have a good trip?'

'Not too bad. A bit bumpy at times. Over the Med, that was.'

'And what did Rikky tell you?'

'Rikky was very unhappy. He's been working like a mule; he's made half a mountain of Mecron, but there's not a hook in it. What he keeps getting is a tranquillizer cum pep pill. You take it, lie down a bit, and in an hour off you go again. You don't come back for it unless you want to. It's just what Hassertons say it is.'

'It's what they're still saying. They're obliged to, aren't they? Once it became public that the Templeton was doing a test they couldn't quietly drop the stuff even if they'd wanted to. Up to then they might have. Remember that the inquiry wasn't originally an official one, and in England when things aren't public they're dealt with unpublicly. The boys get together. They're good at it.'

'What would have happened?'

'The Templeton wouldn't have cooked its report. Latta was trying to, but Latta wasn't typical of scientists. So we had to deal with Latta. No, the Templeton wouldn't have cooked it, but it would probably have discreetly leaked, I dare say with official blessing. Then there'd have been a decent chance for Hassertons to slide out decently. Hassertons are English and they export a lot. I told you this was England.'

The other said, smiling: 'You know more about England than I do.'

'That's my side of the business.'

'Which at the moment is at a standstill. We haven't a grain of Mecron.'

'How long did Rikky say that it would be?'

'He wouldn't guess. Meanwhile we're losing custom—fast. And where we're not losing it the customers get tiresome.'

'How tiresome do they get?'

'In one or two cases, very. One's desperate. He's even threatened us. More Mecron or he'll talk.'

'We might have to deal with him.'

'Like Latta?' A dark head shook emphatically. 'But he's much too important to do quietly. There'd be hell and a bit to pay.'

'So we've got to have more Mecron.'

'Quite. But please tell me how. There were five boxes loose originally, four of them with directors. One of those we got hold of, but the other three were too quick for us. Which left the last with a man called Leggatt. I take it you stole that one?'

'I didn't steal. I bought.'

'You bought?' Black eyebrows rose in alert inquiry. 'You *bought*? You bought Mecron from Henry Leggatt. A Minister of what they call the Crown?'

'I bought it from Mrs. Leggatt. I paid with a private cheque. I took her to the bank with me to pay it in in person. She paid it to a joint account—hers and her husband's.'

There was a considerable silence. Finally the dark man said: 'Smooth. . . . Beautiful, really. But I don't see where it gets us. It'd be lovely if Leggatt had more Mecron, but—'

'There'll be Mecron at the factory still.'

'How do you know?'

'I can't be sure but it's a reasonable bet. There was a week's supply due when they stopped distribution, and I doubt if they worked week to week. There was probably a reserve.'

'A fortnight's production of Mecron would fix us very prettily.'

'So would a lot less. We mustn't be greedy. Or not at first.'

There was another silence before the dark man asked reflectively: 'Henry Leggatt was a director of Hassertons?'

'He was.'

'And Henry Leggatt has a wife? A wife and a joint bank account?'

'He has.'

'He's a Minister of the Crown?'

'For the moment he's a Minister.'

The dark man said obliquely: 'It's lucky women fall for you.' Half-bowing he rose. 'I admit it,' he added, 'you're certainly a professional.'

13

ON MONDAY EVENING Henry was booked for a meeting in his constituency. He held an agreeably safe seat in the West Country, but he had caught himself thinking lately that in various ways he paid for it. He paid for it too highly. But be that as it might be he had to be present that night.

He had returned from the ministry early, changing into the carefully countrified clothes which experience had taught him were acceptable, leaving in the rush hour. He began to walk towards Paddington, not seriously worried that he couldn't find a taxi at once. His suitcase was heavier than usual, for he had a very grand dinner the next evening and an appointment before it where he couldn't appear in the clothes of the gentlemanly tramp which mere constituents were happy with. The top brass of his constituency were a good deal more demanding. So that his suitcase wasn't light—nothing, he decided, breathing a little heavily—nothing which need worry a healthy man. Just the same it wasn't a trifle.

He put it down for a moment, looking again for a taxi. Three passed him engaged, a fourth, and empty, but with the lordly air of the journeyman who had taken enough for one day. And thank you sir, blast your eyes. Henry looked at his watch. He wasn't too worried. He had plenty of time; he could make it still, even walking.

He began to do so briskly, changing his suitcase from hand to hand. It began to seem extraordinarily heavy, and Henry was conscious that he was sweating. He put the suitcase down again, sitting on it, panting now openly. He waved at a couple more taxis but both ignored him; frowning he looked at his watch for the second time. He hadn't as much to spare as he had thought. Deliberately he picked up the suitcase. He broke into a clumsy run.

He had gone thirty paces when he stumbled. The stitch in his side came up at him, sharp and inescapable. It wasn't a boy's stitch, an uncomfortable preliminary to a second wind, but final, a clawing agony. It stopped him in his tracks, crippled and gasping.

Henry put down the suitcase again, this time against a wall, sitting on it, ignoring stares. God, he was out of condition. And he had got to get to Lynchester. There was a public meeting tonight, one with his agent tomorrow, another with the committee, dinner with the Harte-Robinsons. . . .

He found himself thinking about Lynchester, looking behind him at his reflection in a shop window. He decided he looked terrible. It wouldn't do to appear in Lynchester looking like catsmeat. They'd put it down to drink and worse.

. . . Lynchester—what a dump! And he'd a meeting that same evening: once he arrived in Lynchester he'd be hopelessly committed. He thought about the meeting soberly. It wouldn't count politically, for Lynchester was the sort of constituency where the real decisions would be taken at the Harte-Robinsons' dreadful dinner table, but any meeting was public relations, a formal appearance whether you liked it or not. The Member would be on the platform, the second-flight worthies round him. The worthies did the solid work but five families rode the constituency. The Member, too if he wasn't damned careful. The worthies had social ambitions. Sometimes they made it, more often they didn't, but the Harte-Robinsons kept the say-so.

It was that sort of constituency, a nice safe seat.

Still, any meeting was always important. It was a public appearance, in this case much too public. He couldn't afford to risk it when he looked like death. They might be the second eleven but they had remarkably sharp eyes. Henry could see the dreary hall for he'd been in it fifty times. He'd be up on the platform and the lighting would be merciless. The hall would be in darkness but he could see the first six rows. Women they'd be, or nearly all of them, very much ladies in tweeds and neat wool twin sets, ladies in pearls, not all of them false. They'd watch him unwaveringly, passing polite asides, not moving their heads and only just their lips. They'd be terribly well-bred. Later they'd question him. They'd ask him where he stood on blood sports, NATO, the bomb, the whip. Oh, certainly the lash. They'd bay for flogging like a pack of hounds. The Thursday pack at that. Bitches. He couldn't face them.

He found a taxi at last, directing it to the nearest post office. There he sent a telegram, apologetic but not excessively, leaving to stand for a moment with a foot on the taxi's platform. Finally he made up his mind; he told the driver to take him to a house in Regent's Park. He'd never before been there but he had heard of it more than once. It sounded what he wanted.

But his stomach sank a little as an immaculate manservant admitted him, more in the waiting-room. This wasn't a place for beginners but the temple of a serious cult. At last a Japanese came in. He was even more impeccable than the manservant—white collar, black coat and beautiful houndstooth trousers. He said in an English which matched his clothes:

'Can I help you, sir?'

'I want to get fit again.' Henry hadn't meant to blurt it out. He saw at once that he had blundered.

The polite Japanese face hardened. 'We're not quite for that, you know.'

'I know. But I thought . . .'

'There are places called Health Clubs.'

'I couldn't stand a Health Club.'

'Or even gymnasia.'

Gymnasia, Henry thought, went perfectly with sponge-bag trousers.

'They're not the same thing. They've no—no tradition.' Henry was watching the Japanese, and for a moment he seemed appeased. Henry followed his advantage. 'My name is Henry Leggatt. I'm a Member of Parliament.' He was despising himself, but he was deadly keen. 'Actually I'm a Minister—Parliamentary Secretary in the Ministry of Social Welfare.'

He saw that it had turned the trick. The Japanese bowed again, this time lower by a calculated inch.

'Have you any knowledge of Judo? Any previous experience?'

'Strictly speaking, no. But I did a good deal of unarmed combat in the war.'

'Ah yes. *Kime-no-Kata* and the fifteen throws. The crudest self-defence, of course.' The Japanese wasn't contemptuous but simply matter-of-fact. He spoke as a Test cricketer might have mentioned some casual fifty on a village green.

'It might be something to start from.'

'Indeed. We have one or two beginners, a few in the *kyu* grades. But very, very few.' The Japanese smiled blandly. 'We're a finishing school, really. We'd find it difficult to fit you in.'

'If you could try. . . .'

The Japanese considered; at last he walked to the door, holding it open for Henry. 'Come with me, please,' he said.

He led the way into a cool, bare room, its floor covered with the classic *tatami*. In the opposite wall was an inconspicuous door. The Japanese opened it in turn. 'You'll find clean clothes. Be so good as to change.' He bowed again. 'I too will change.'

Henry found trousers and a jacket. There was a selection of belts and he took one. He knew enough to choose a white.

When he returned the Japanese was awaiting him. Henry saw that he was a high, high Dan. He was silent for perhaps ten seconds, staring at Henry reflectively. Finally he said, still courteous: 'You *have* got a good deal of flesh. I would still suggest that massage, a little gentle exercise. . . . In a month or two perhaps. . . .'

'I'd never keep it up.'

'As you wish.' The Japanese shrugged faintly. 'You tell

me you're not quite ignorant. I'd like to see you fall, please. Just an ordinary side breakfall.'

Henry, feeling foolish, did an ordinary side breakfall.

'Not too bad. I can see you've been taught. Now a rolling breakfall, please. Left to right.'

Henry did a rolling breakfall, left to right.

The Japanese was evidently pleased. 'I confess I've seen much worse. *Much* worse. Now again, please—six of each. Continuous.'

Henry did a dozen, continuous. He was sweating like a horse.

'Good. Now throw me, please.' The Japanese made the formal Judo bow, saying something which Henry didn't understand. He added in English: 'Simple trip and hip throw. . . . Now.'

The Japanese went down like a feather. Henry had pulled a muscle.

'Now I'll throw *you*.'

'All right.'

There was a frightful crash.

'Bad, very bad. You can breakfall all right, as an exercise, I mean, but you fall very badly in *randori*.' The Japanese looked at Henry again. Henry was steaming and a little sick. 'That's enough for one day, I think. I'll show you the baths and I'll send you the masseur. I observe you could use one.' For the first time the Dan became human; he said almost shyly: 'You—you interest me, sir.'

Henry took a bath, and afterwards the manservant, stripped to the waist, did painful but somehow soothing things to back and limbs. Later in the upstairs room, the Japanese was waiting for him. 'We shall be pleased,' he said.

'I don't know how to thank you.'

'Come often. Try hard.'

'I'll come tomorrow.'

The Japanese looked doubtful. 'Tomorrow you'll be very stiff.'

'Then better to work it off.'

'Let us say the day after.'

'I'll come then too.'

The Japanese said something in his own language again, apologizing at once. 'It was a proverb,' he explained.

'Something about overdoing it? Fools rushing in . . . ?'

'Not at all. I was thinking that you were a serious man.' For a second the Dan hesitated. 'A glutton for punishment,' he said.

Henry took another taxi, dining at his unpretentious club, eating alone in thought. Events had forced on him a decision which privately he had been ducking. He must decide things with Patricia, and finally.

He would have admitted that the excuses to postpone a crisis hadn't been unwelcome. For there had been excuses, pretexts of time. It had been Saturday morning when he had discovered that his wife had accepted five hundred pounds of another man's money, and in the immediate encounter which had followed she had first wrong-footed him, then fatally lost him his temper. Then she had left London for one of her country Sundays—houses in Surrey and Sussex, he thought, the stockbroker belt of Hampshire. How the wen spread. And this evening he should have been away himself, touting in a constituency the thought of which had begun to offend him. But now he'd be at home; he couldn't decline combat and look himself in the face, since tomorrow Patricia was leaving again, and this time for several days. Not to one of her fancy friends but to Lord Egham's Durham fastness. She was a distant Egham—he'd never known the precise relationship—but an Egham she'd been born. And once a year the marquess held an enormous house party; once a year the preposterous old palace came to life again. It pleased the old man to sit in feudal state, the clan around him. He couldn't afford it but he didn't care. He was Lord Egham still. He didn't invite Mr. Henry Leggatt, but Henry wasn't resentful. He wasn't an Egham.

Indeed he was not. Henry sighed softly into a pint of bitter beer. It had been forty-eight hours, a little more, since he'd been to his bank, and it seemed a great deal longer. And tomorrow Patricia would be away again. He couldn't with decency postpone the inevitable.

He was back in the flat by ten, and Patricia met him with a surprise which she did nothing to conceal.

'I thought you were in the constituency.'

'I found I couldn't face it.'

'I don't understand.'

'Let's say that I suddenly saw them—sitting there, asking me damn fool questions. Smug as a row of well-fed cats. Which, come to think of it, they are.'

'It's your life, of course. Politics.' Her shrug was the slightest but its meaning evident. It disassociated Henry Leggatt's wife from politics.

'Not all of it,' he said.

She didn't answer him.

'The rest of it's rather a mess. There's that five hundred pounds.' He looked round the room, his senses unwontedly sharp. There was nothing he could point to, no hat, no stick, no tell-tale cigar butt. There wouldn't be, he thought—there wouldn't be anything vulgar. But there was the impalpable presence of another man. It was fading but it was there still. Patricia had had company.

She sat down resignedly. 'I suppose you'll talk sometime.'

He said in a voice which surprised him, crisp and edged: 'Thank you, I'm talking now. You took five hundred of Dick Asher's money. Why?'

'But I told you. We were hopelessly in debt and I sold him some Mecron.'

'For five hundred pounds? Two gross of tubes?'

'I guessed it might be a lot. It's nine and six in the shops. I don't know what it costs you but I assume you make a profit.' She said profit in a tone he recognized. People like Patricia lived on profits, other people's at that, but they had a special way of saying it. To people like Patricia profit was a faintly dirty word.

He didn't rise to it: instead he said evenly: 'So you knew it was much too much?'

126

'I don't deny I guessed it.'

'And you knew where I stood with Mecron? The politics—my old firm, the row in the House?'

'Henry, be sensible. Who'll ever find out?'

'It wouldn't be difficult if anybody wanted to. There's been five hundred pounds in our joint account and it came from a cheque of Asher's.'

'And who's going to pry into Dick Asher's bank account?'

'Anybody interested in Mecron. Anybody interested in what he does with two gross of tubes of it.'

She said too quickly: 'The police?'

'Why should it be the police?'

'But *I* was asking.' She was trying to recover.

He said quite truthfully: 'I suspect things about Dick Asher and quite soon I expect to be sure. But I know, really know, almost nothing about him. Except that he has a good deal of money and no regular job to earn it. You can add that to what you like.'

'I add it to nothing,' she said.

'What do *you* know about him?'

'He's very good company and he does have money. His friends are the same as mine.'

'He hasn't any others?'

'Not that I know of.' Her back straightened suddenly 'Have you finished the inquisition?'

'Not quite. . . . Why did you go to the bank? With Asher, I mean.'

'Does it matter?'

'It matters to me; it matters to me personally. I'm a pretty junior Minister whom you've probably destroyed, but I'm not sure I mind it. It's queer. But I'm also your husband. I'm an ordinary male with the ordinary male's distaste for looking abject. . . . Why did you go to the bank with him?'

'It was part of the five hundred.'

'You'll have to explain.'

But she laughed. 'It wasn't five hundred to start with. I pushed him up a bit. I haggled. I'm not middle-class, you know, so I don't mind bargaining. In the end he said that if I would go to the bank with him he'd make it five hundred.'

'And still you went.'

'There was two hundred difference.'

'You were seen there, you know. You were recognized.'

'I guessed that was what he wanted.' She was perfectly cool still.

'Then you must have known why he wanted it.'

'I—I wasn't sure.' For the first time her self-possession wasn't quite absolute. 'I really didn't think.'

'But it couldn't have been as *evidence*, could it? If he'd been thinking of destroying me politically the cheque would have done alone.'

'I didn't think of that. Evidence. . . . I'm not a lawyer. I think you're making a mountain out of a molehill.'

'That I shall know quite soon.'

His voice was grim and Patricia caught it. She rose, standing for a moment in an uncertainty Henry had never seen in her. At last she said: 'Then that's about all, I think. I must go and do my packing.'

He heard himself ask calmly: 'Will you be coming back?'

'I—I honestly don't know. I've been meaning to think it over.'

'I'd be glad if you'd do that.'

Mr. Robert Seneschal had waited nearly a week since his interview with the Prime Minister, but not because he hadn't understood its meaning. He was more than intelligent enough to have known from six sentences that he was in serious trouble. It was the fact that he was so which had astonished him. To Seneschal himself astonishment would have been too mild a word, but whatever the word the fact remained. He was over a barrel and knew it.

For it was inescapable that he had miscalculated, and in politics misjudgements were fatal. He had seen the affair of Mecron as a logical proposition: the party was worried about how it was developing, there'd been a row in the House which the Home Secretary had muffed, and further pressure was inevitable though he didn't know when or how. And that was a situation which he had seen as potentially to his advantage. Indeed what had troubled him was the possibility that he might act too soon. You got no thanks for stepping in too soon and certainly no advancement. He'd have to time it sensibly, let it get worse, oh yes, a good deal worse. It wasn't enough that the Home Secretary was embarrassed: the party must be deep in it too. He must wait till it was serious, just short of crisis, then. . . .

Then he'd step in, the deus ex machina, saviour. He wasn't without a plan, and when Number Ten had telephoned his decision of time had been taken for him. He'd fixed the interview for three o'clock, but by five past three he'd known that he wasn't a saviour. On the contrary if he wasn't very careful he'd be scapegoat.

He realized that he had somewhere slipped. It rankled. He knew that he had done so once before, the matter of the back-benchers who had unexpectedly but fatally bristled over a matter where an intelligent man could take only one view. And naturally that had been Seneschal's. But for that misfortune—he wouldn't admit to error—Robert Seneschal would have been Prime Minister himself—well, Home Secretary at least. Instead he was stuck with Social Welfare, but he was still immensely useful to the party. His aura, his public smell, was worth a mint of votes. He wasn't by any means finished, and a coup over Mecron, a private and unofficial coup which in forty-eight hours everybody in the party would know about, would put him right back in the running. Robert would be the blue-eyed boy.

It had been neat, very pretty, and Seneschal resented that it seemed to have been quite wrong. In fact he'd misjudgd two factors: the nature of politics, the politics of his party, and the Prime Minister as a politician. For the Prime Minister hadn't received him as a saviour; he'd received him as a potential rival still, one who had already meddled with Mecron and was therefore committed to handle it better next time. And quickly at that. The Prime Minister hadn't said meddled but he had perfectly conveyed it. . . . Henry Leggatt was Mr. Seneschal's Parliamentary Secretary, was he not? And Mr. Leggatt had once been employed by Hassertons who made Mecron? Yes? But wasn't that rather, well, rather a *tenuous* connection for Social Welfare to have interested itself in a matter which was clearly for the Home Office? To have approached the Templeton, to have arranged delay with Hassertons through Leggatt, an ex-director? Of course it hadn't been a bad idea: it might have worked and well.

It was a pity it simply hadn't. It was a pity, for instance, that *The Gong* was considering another splash. By the technical standards of journalism *The Gong* was a very good newspaper, but it hadn't the reputation of continuous policy. Yesterday's headline was tomorrow's shroud, and when *The Gong* ran things twice a wise politician looked for cover. . . . How did the Prime Minister know that *The Gong* . . . ? Mr. Seneschal must forgive him. And the Prime Minister also knew that the Opposition was cooking something: the tribal stoves were stewing smokily. Well, there it was. A pity it hadn't worked the first time. Bad luck in a way. Mr. Seneschal's very real services. . . . But politics were politics and the unwritten rules. . . .

The Prime Minister hadn't used the phrase nor anything as banal. But it had been visible over his shoulder, a writing on a highly political wall.

Robert Seneschal had left the interview both miserable and furious, since privately he had never accepted something his colleagues took for granted. It was the fact that in politics intelligence wasn't everything. There were even people who mistrusted it. Seneschal wasn't one of them. He had a first-class brain, he was four times more intelligent than the Prime Minister. He ought to go to the top in politics, he had a *right* to. Instead that second-rate Prime Minister, a manager, no more, simply a high-class fixer—the clown was going to break him.

Or would if he didn't pull one.

Seneschal had thought it over for a week. He didn't like it that the interview hadn't been quite alone. The Prime Minister was too accomplished to hold that sort of interview with another Minister present, but Lord Egham had been there, massive and wholly silent. And Lord Egham was the party's conscience. Seneschal knew what that meant. When Lord Egham was in waiting it wasn't simply politics; certainly it wasn't administration. Lord Egham was the party, the backbenchers and just how far an enlightened man like Seneschal could drag them, the ageless, unshaken roots. Lord Egham hadn't been there for nothing. He had sat in total silence, splendidly bearded, his soft hound's eyes staring at Robert Seneschal. He was a totem but not a soft one. Without a word spoken he had defined the position perfectly, and he had saved a discussion of Henry Leggatt. For Henry Leggatt was married to a distant Egham. Not that the distance mattered: she was an Egham. The warning had come through perfectly. It wouldn't be Leggatt resigning: ditching Henry Leggatt wouldn't work. Egham wouldn't wear it.

So there it was, a political sleigh, and the wolves were uncomfortably close. If they couldn't be driven off, dispersed without a scandal. . . .

Robert Seneschal had made few friends; he wouldn't be much regretted. The Prime Minister in particular wouldn't regret him at all. The Prime Minister still thought of him as dangerous.

For a moment the reflection cheered him. If he were a rival still there must be a reason. And that was obvious: he was still extremely useful to the party, plenty of people voted for it who would have run screaming from its embraces if it hadn't had Robert Seneschal. Why, he had practically won an election; he was an image.

. . . And suppose they had decided that a newer one was better, a new look Robert Seneschal? That Leggatt was very good, more popular on telly and more—more colloquial.

. . . Lord Egham again.

Robert Seneschal frowned. He'd been thinking for nearly a week and now he must act. Events had moved against him too. Latta was inconveniently dead, and he couldn't talk to the Templeton laboratory. Not as he had talked to Latta. He didn't dare.

He reviewed his hand, disliking it.

Well, there was always bluff.

14

HENRY WOKE THREE days later, conscious of a sensation which he hadn't felt for years, the spur and goad of energy. He was too realistic to imagine that he was wholly a fit man again: four bouts of Judo could hardly have done that, but there were symptoms of a returning physical sanity. The coffee he made himself smelt wonderful: he could taste, but really taste, the cigarette he smoked with it. He shaved and dressed, whistling almost blithely. His trousers, he noticed, were the least bit too big for him. It was nothing remarkable, but four monstrous sweatings hadn't been ineffective. He pulled his belt in by a single hole. There were several to go before he could tell himself that he was trim again, but undeniably he'd lost an inch. And that reminded him: he must go easy on drinks and starches. They'd dropped him a courteous hint about the starches.

At Piccadilly Circus he decided to walk the rest. It was a cold, clear morning and the exercise wouldn't hurt him. More important, he felt like walking. Not to put a point on it he felt better than he had felt for years. It was as well he did since he had a trying day in wait for him.

It began with a note on his desk: Mr. Seneschal would like to see him as soon as he arrived. The note was in Seneschal's own writing and, though he hadn't been conscious of it, he had somehow implied that if the Minister could arrive by a quarter to ten his junior should have done so.

Henry walked along the corridor to Seneschal's room.

'Come in.'

Henry went in. Seneschal offered him a chair and the morning cup of tea. Henry took the chair but not the tea, for tea at ten in the morning wasn't one of his vices. In any case

Seneschal's secretary made terrible tea. Seneschal said deliberately: 'I wanted to talk to you.'

'Here I am.'

Seneschal looked faintly surprised. 'Here I am' wasn't an answer which Henry Leggatt had previously given him, and there was something about the tone of voice, an unaccustomed bite, almost as though they had been equals, almost as though Leggatt knew that Seneschal was in peril. Mr. Seneschal shook his head. He didn't put it beyond the Prime Minister to have conveyed a hint to Leggatt; he'd have done so without scruple if he'd seen an advantage, but no, there would hardly be one. Henry Leggatt had married an Egham and old Egham had been present at the interview, but Leggatt was still small beer—too small to be worth hinting to. The explanation was simpler: the junior Minister was getting above himself. He, Robert Seneschal, would have to slap him down.

If he could, he thought uneasily.

'It's about Mecron, of course.'

'Oh yes? Has something brewed up again?'

Robert Seneschal began to talk and Henry listened carefully. He couldn't make head or tail of it. Seneschal wanted him to do something—that much was obvious—but what it might really be he hadn't an inkling. Seneschal talked in allusions—hints, innuendoes; Seneschal was a shocking bore. Henry let him finish, half-attending; then he asked simply:

'What do you want me to do?'

There was immediate silence. Seneschal ordered more tea and both men reflected. Henry was thinking that he wasn't afraid of Seneschal. He knew that once he had been. That put it too high perhaps, but not entirely. Seneschal's good opinion of him had been important: in a sense he'd been dependent on him. And now he wasn't. If he took a decision which he had more than half taken he'd be shot of Robert Seneschal, shot of the whole damned pack of them. It wouldn't be easy, naturally. He was forty-four and he could hardly go back to Hassertons; he'd have to start from scratch again. Not that he needed much money, since he'd been accustomed to it only for a year or two and it hadn't conditioned him. There were a dozen things which colleagues seemed to find essential which to Henry were still luxuries. And he did have a skill— he could sell things. He'd start at rock bottom if he had to, door-to-door knockings, gate-to-gate slammings. But he wouldn't do that for long. He was a good salesman and not ashamed of it, and in a country where selling still wasn't quite work for gentlemen that was a marketable skill. And if you were good with foreigners the sky was the limit. Even at forty-four.

But Seneschal was speaking and he sounded pained. ·

'That puts it a little crudely.' ·

'You could call me a crude man.'

Robert Seneschal didn't answer. Politics were his life; he couldn't afford to leave them, especially under a cloud. His wife was a rich woman, she gave him food and houseroom in the hideous Dorset mansion, she was flattered by his position; but she wasn't his wife. Her husband was still his predecessor, rich, extrovert and male. Four sons there were, and Seneschal didn't like them; he thought them uncultured, and he didn't much care for their manner with him. It lacked— well, it wasn't exactly respectful. They were stockbrokers, merchants, men in Lloyd's—barbarians, he privately considered, all four of them. It wasn't surprising that Robert Seneschal had a house but not a home. Not that Helen wasn't kind to him, even generous. Recently he'd tried a little farming and Helen had financed it. He'd farmed in the most enlightened way, improving the breed of this, the yield of that. He'd read a great deal and he'd been wholly confident. It had shaken him when fourteen months of scientific farming had lost him ten thousand pounds.

Or rather had lost Helen. She hadn't been pleased. He knew that she would carry him, but only just so far. She'd pay for his hobbies—a man must have a hobby—but under the goodfellowship was a very shrewd woman. A Minister was worth pocket money, worth his discreet amusements, but ten thousand pounds was a little too close for comfort to an unspoken limit.

. . . And if he wasn't a Minister?

Robert Seneschal said heavily: 'Mecron.'

'We started from Mecron.' Henry's own voice surprised him. It sounded patient.

'I'd like you to go to Hassertons. To get them to drop it.' Seneschal had dragged it out reluctantly. These weren't words which he could later disown or gloss; they were unequivocal, one-meaning sentences. He had taken a position, he was finally committed.

He hated it.

He heard Henry laugh and stared at him incredulous. The man was laughing at him.

'You find something funny?'

'I'm sorry.' The words asked indulgence but not the tone. 'I do.'

Seneschal said stiffly: 'My own sense of humour—'

'It isn't a question of humour but of fact. I *could* go to Hassertons. I could even ask them to do what you suggest. And why do you think they should?'

'They're a most reputable firm. A reputable firm in trouble over a proprietary product.'

'It hasn't been established.'

'It may well be. They're running a considerable risk.'

'Of course they are—we forced the risk on them. You remember our little arrangement? There was nothing in that about the Home Secretary making a public statement in the House. *The Gong* obliged us to do that, and I dare say Hassertons realized it. They didn't complain—they're not the complaining kind—but we've stuck them with Mecron for better or worse.'

'They might drop it even now to—to save you.'

'And why should they do that? It was me you sent to blackmail them.'

'I don't like that word.'

'I don't like that thing. In any case I'm not going to ask a favour of Hassertons. I'd rather die.'

'Politically you may.' Mr. Seneschal was portentous. He had decided to bluff and he intended to do it properly. He contrived to sound very severe.

'Oh, that again. But I told you before. I'm an ex-director of Hassertons and there's trouble about Mecron. I can see that's very awkward. But I told you I'd resign, and meant it. I dare say you didn't believe me—plenty wouldn't. But I'll write it out now if you like.'

'I don't think it would help us.'

'Why not? Aren't I big enough meat for the wolves?'

There was silence again, wholly unexpected. Henry stared at Robert Seneschal. He was white as a new tombstone. Henry had spoken without other thought; he hadn't been probing. But now he knew he'd hit one, a raw tense nerve. He rose embarrassed, ashamed for Robert Seneschal. 'Then that's about all, I think. But I'll be in my room.'

As he walked down the corridor he whistled softly. Robert Seneschal was up against the wall. It wasn't explained but it wasn't mistakable. Henry had seen that face before and the firing squad had been loading.

That evening he walked back to Dorset Square from Regent's Park. He was pleasantly tired but not exhausted, and an evening alone was something he was looking forward to. He had plenty to think about.

He had taken a cautious whisky, stirring most of the gas from the soda, when the front door bell rang. Henry sighed but he opened, and Dick Asher said coolly: 'May I come in?'

'I don't see why not. I was rather expecting you.'

Asher sat down, perfectly at ease. 'If you were expecting me we needn't beat about the bush. I can put things very simply.'

'I'd be glad if you did. I spent the morning with the opposite.'

'Indeed?' Asher wasn't interested in Henry's morning. 'Then I want something from you.'

'That much I'd guessed. It's money of course. You won't get it.'

'It's not money at all. I want something called Mecron.'

'I don't have any Mecron—not any more. That you must know.'

'I do.'

'Then you're being less clear than you promised.'

'There's Mecron at the factory still.'

'It wouldn't surprise me.'

'You're going to get me some.'

Henry said with a dangerous quietness: 'I am? And how do you suggest?'

'I don't suggest. The detail, the method, is up to you. You're an ex-director and you're a Minister of the Crown. A Minister on a spot.'

'I know. You put me there.' Henry considered; he might as well know everything. 'May I ask why?'

'It was business. I'm interested in Mecron professionally.'

'That much I'd realized. I don't think it was all, though.'

'You don't? Well, it wasn't.' Asher had been very quiet but now he flared suddenly. 'You can't think I like you. And it isn't only personal. I don't like your party. I hate what it stands for. I hate what it's done to me—to us. I hate its guts.'

'I'm not sure I like it myself. Or not any more. . . .'

There was a Mediterranean gesture. Henry ignored it.

'. . . Not that I expect you to believe me. In any case it's not the point.'

'No.' Asher was impersonal again. 'The point is that I have you cold. You've got to produce more Mecron or . . .' The shrug that followed wasn't theatrical. 'I don't care how you do it, what weapons you use with Hassertons. You can plead, you can threaten if you've anything to threaten with, you can steal for all I care. But you're going to get me Mecron.'

'You sound very sure of it.'

'I am. I told you I had you cold.'

'It was clever, I admit it. I know all about it by now. You took her to the bank with you to make quite sure. It pleases me she made you pay for that. Two hundred extra, wasn't it?'

For the scintilla of a second Dick Asher hesitated. It was something which only a good stopwatch could have measured, but Henry noticed it. He looked up suddenly, and for an instant Asher's face was blank. But he recovered very quickly. 'Yes,' he said. 'Oh, yes.'

Henry held his eyes. 'She pushed you to five hundred?'

'Five hundred I paid. Does the price matter? A lot less would have fixed you.'

'The price was three hundred, wasn't it? The extra was for going to the bank with you.'

'Of course,' Asher said. He laughed, for the first time not wholly confident. It was almost imperceptible. 'A very good business woman, Mrs. Leggatt."

'You're pretty quick at covering.'

'I don't understand you.'

'You're not meant to understand. But you've told me something—something important.' Henry rose with decision. 'And now,' he said, 'get out.'

'You're being very foolish. You haven't a hope, you know.'

'You think I'm a fool?'

'I'm sure of it. We—'

'Perhaps I am. I know I've been one. Thank you for that.' Henry walked to the door, holding it open. 'Out,' he said crisply. 'Scram.'

Dick Asher shrugged but Dick Asher got up. At the door he said venomously: 'I'll be back. *We'll* be back.'

'You'll be wasting your time.'

'They always say that.'

Henry went into the dressing-room, turning on the bath. . . . Patricia had never lied to him—he'd clung to that pathetically. And now she had. She'd wanted the money, she'd admitted that, but the story of a bargain had been a calculated lie. He'd seen Asher's face: Dick Asher hadn't known what he was talking about. Asher had covered quickly but he'd given it away. She'd simply betrayed him—sold him and knowingly, a party to bitter malice. It had been five

139

hundred pounds all along, all the conditions known and all the implications. They'd have talked it over, laughing. Asher wouldn't have deceived her since he didn't need to try. Patricia was accomplice, not a stooge.

And of course she was his mistress. She'd all but admitted it, but subconsciously he'd fought it. Now. . . .

Now that didn't seem important.

He climbed into the bath, washing very carefully, feet, crutch and hair, like a gipsy, he thought, a gipsy after touching death. Normally he lay long in baths, soaking the heat up, half asleep; but from this one he jumped quickly, washing the bath in turn. He took a shower afterwards, towelling his head furiously, humming. What he was humming surprised him. It was an air from a popular musical and he hadn't been conscious that it was apposite. But he'd have to change the genders. He wasn't a woman and it wasn't a man he was washing away. Right out of his hair. But that apart it suited perfectly. It was queer how these things came up at you. Sometime he'd consider it, but not just now. He didn't want to think; he was content to feel, and what he felt was clean again.

He put on a dressing-gown, ringing Rachel Borrodaile at her flat. 'It's started,' he said. 'Asher came this evening.' He began to explain but she cut him short.

'Come round and tell me. Have you eaten?'

'No, not yet.'

'I'll give you a meal.'

'I don't want to trouble you. I—'

'Give me a quick half-hour.'

She put the receiver down firmly, starting to change her shoes. She had been in slippers and it was raining. She chose sensible shoes for walking, flatties, clucking in irritation as she saw that they weren't a pair. One, she remembered, she'd sent for mending. She found others and a mackintosh, walking quickly to a delicatessen. She bought crab, ready dressed, tomatoes and fresh lettuce, a long loaf of elegant bread. Wine and cheese she already had. They were her usual supper.

She returned to the flat and the little kitchen, hesitating.

Henry would expect potatoes, and he shouldn't be eating them, but to deny him would be churlish, the sort of hint a woman shouldn't give. Finally she shrugged. At least he should have them properly cooked. She began to do so carefully, drying them meticulously, making sure that the fat was smoking. The English addiction to potatoes was something she still deplored, but these smelt delicious.

The bell interrupted her and she went to the door still aproned. Henry said apologetically: 'I'm afraid I'm a terrible nuisance.'

'Only when you excuse yourself.' She gave him a drink. 'Help yourself when you've finished that one.'

'One'll be plenty, thanks.'

'Then I'll be back in ten minutes.'

In fact it was a little more, for she had not only cooked but changed discreetly. She could see he was admiring her. They ate in a little alcove off the even smaller kitchen. 'There's a dining-room,' she said. 'I never use it.'

'It's very nice here.' Henry looked round the little room. 'I like the pictures.'

'I'm not at all knowledgeable. I buy what I like.'

'And I like what you buy.' He began to tell her about Dick Asher, but she stopped him.

'We'll talk about that later.' She looked at his glass, his plate. 'Won't you have some potato?'

'They tempt me to death but I'm off potato.'

'You look the better for it.' She could see she had pleased him.

'You really think so?'

'Indeed I do. You look fitter than I've seen you look for days.'

He laughed and she liked the sound of it. 'I've been taking a bit of exercise. I needed it.'

'What sort of exercise?'

'Oh,' Henry said, 'just exercise.'

Rachel was curious but didn't press it. She accepted his compliments on the salad dressing she had mixed herself and, with the cheese, she let him talk again.

141

'Asher's been round. He came to put the bite on.'

'What did he want?' But she knew the answer.

'Not money,' he said, 'or not directly. He wanted Mecron —Mecron from the factory. I was to get Mecron from Hassertons or. . . .' His shrug mimicked Asher's. 'He had it all pat; he had me and knew it. He couldn't have been franker. Patricia, that cheque, the bank. . . .'

She saw him flush and saved him. 'What did you tell him?'

'I told him to go to hell.'

'Just about all you could do. Not that it helps, of course.' She looked at him squarely. 'You're not out of the wood. You're not really even in it.'

'I know.'

'He'll come again. Oh yes, he'll come again.'

He asked quietly: 'And not alone?'

'It's possible.' Rachel had answered soberly. 'Henry, have you a weapon?'

'I've an old thirty-eight but not the bullets.'

'I'll send you some,' she said. 'It's shockingly illegal but I might as well jump right in.'

'Right into what?'

'Right into Henry Leggatt. I'm not the Executive, or not in this. I'm only Rachel Borrodaile. I could put a man on your flat without reporting it, but sooner or later somebody would get curious. Which wouldn't be good for you. Because I haven't told Russell a word. I haven't dared.'

She watched him think it over. At last he said: 'I can't accept that you should risk your job, I can't accept—'

'Be quiet.'

'I won't agree—'

'Shut up.'

He laughed unexpectedly. 'You're a very nice woman,' he said. He saw her flush in turn and wondered why. He had forgotten about good scouts.

Later they went upstairs again and Rachel made coffee. Presently Henry looked at his watch. The time surprised him.

'It's almost midnight.'

She went to the door with him and on the doorstep he

hesitated. He began to thank her again but she cut him short.

'You're looking extremely fit.'

She knew that she'd astonished him. She'd meant to.

'You said that before.'

'I know. And it's true.' It was true, she was thinking. He had something she'd known before, courage again, and the hint of an imperative masculinity.

He said, but not imperatively: 'But I mean . . . as I'm leaving . . . on the doorstep. . . .'

'It's you on the doorstep.'

She wasn't offended that he considered it. Some men were much too quick and she'd grown very tired of them.

'Don't stand there like a schoolboy.'

Henry Leggatt took the door from her. He went into the flat again.

15

THE ROOM IN Camden Town was a good deal fuller than usual, blue with tobacco smoke, smelling faintly of foreign foods. There was wine on the table and most men were drinking it sparingly. There wasn't a drop of spirits. The air was electric with the unmistakable stress of crisis. The dark man was speaking and he seemed to be summing up.

'So there it is. The last lot you gave us was useless. It no more had a hook in it than anything of Rikky's. That's bad, very bad. Unsatisfied customers get tiresome, but a swindled customer gets something a good deal worse. By my book he's a right to.' The dark man looked around him. 'I dare say we're most sort of scoundrel but we've never sold sugar and said it was snow. That wrecks any business known. And this is a good one, or was.' He faced Dick Asher deliberately. 'Well, there it is. Next move to you.'

'I've made it—I told you last time. There's Mecron at the factory still and Leggatt's an ex-director. I've enough strings on Leggatt to hang him a dozen times.'

'You've talked to him—put the bite on?'

'Yes.'

A bald man in the corner stood up suddenly. 'Then where's the Mecron?' The bald man didn't sit down again.

Dick Asher looked round the room in turn. An experienced committee-man, Robert Seneschal for instance, would have sensed at once that the meeting was slipping. It wasn't yet out of control, but the chairman wasn't popular. He'd have a job to hold it.

But the bald man was talking again. He was speaking in Greek and it wasn't very good. Somebody said tolerantly: 'You've been here too long. Speak English if you must.'

'Okay, I will.' The bald man turned to Asher. 'I'd like to get this straight. You've been to see this Leggatt?"
'Yes.'
'You don't much like him, do you? You'd like to smash him personally.'
'What's that to do with it?'
'A lot. Perhaps too much. You're always telling us this is a business. So you go to see Leggatt on business but we don't see any Mecron.' The bald man's eyebrows rose. 'I suppose he stalled on it.'
'He did. They often stall at first. It takes a little time.'
'Time's just what we can't afford. Nor personal dislikes.' The bald man held his hand up as a dozen voices drowned him. There was immediate and respectful silence for the bald man was a killer with a killer's standing. 'Listen to me. I'm tired of peddling Mecron for pennies. It was worth it to keep the market open, worth it as long as Rikky was going to make proper supplies for us. But Rikky's a broken reed; Rikky hasn't made an ounce of Mecron with a hook in it. We're asked to believe he will, but it'll be accident if he does. There's something *about* this stuff.' The bald man drank some wine and nobody interrupted him. The room was very still. When his glass was finished the bald man went on steadily. 'And meanwhile there's a dump of it at the factory. You told us so. Perhaps all of it isn't good Mecron—good in our sense—but it's long odds that some of it will be. And that'd be a killing, an immediate certain killing. There's no future in Rikky—nothing to rely on. But it's there at the factory, waiting for us, a straightforward once-for-all job. At our sort of prices that'd be well worth while. Never mind about Rikky, forget about the future. I'm sick and tired of waiting.'
There was an ominous murmur, then silence again. Into it Asher said:
'You're crazy. This is England.'
'We've heard plenty about England—much too much. I don't care where it is.'
'Then suppose it's where you like. How are you going to work it? There's a factory covering acres and we'd be looking

145

for a single drug. Hassertons make everything. We haven't a map, we haven't a guide—'

'Oh yes, we have.'

The silence now was palpable. They were listening to the bald man, wanting to listen. 'Go on,' Asher said.

'We've your dear friend Henry Leggatt, the one you were going to blackmail, the one who called you. Henry Leggatt's an ex-director and directors know their factories. Not perfectly perhaps, but quite enough for us.'

The dark man joined in again, saying reflectively: 'You'd take him along? You'd—well, persuade him?'

'I'd bring him here first for that.'

'He sounds fairly tough. He stood up to Asher.'

'But that's just the point. He stood up to threats, to words. I'm tired of words, Asher's or anyone else's.' The bald man showed superlative white teeth again, nudging the man beside him. 'Remember that German Colonel? A full Colonel at that, eyeglass and all of it. Very haughty he was. At first. He lasted just seven minutes.' The bald man pointed suddenly. 'You—Alexis?'

'Yes.'

'Argenti?'

'Yes.'

'Thivaios?'

'Count me in.'

Dick Asher said furiously: 'You haven't a hope in hell. Half-planned and ill-considered violence. There are a dozen objections. First—'

'First we'll get moving.' The bald man was smiling, masterful, certain of mastery.

Dick Asher shrugged. 'I want no part of this.'

The bald man stared at him, and now he wasn't smiling.

'Oh yes, you do. You do indeed.'

16

CHARLES RUSSELL WAS walking back from lunch at the Mandarins. It hadn't been his intention to eat there, but it had begun to drizzle unexpectedly, and it had been a nice decision between unrolling his beautiful umbrella, going on to his other club, or facing the indifferent Mandarin menu. He had chosen the latter.

Now he was glad he had. He thought of the Mandarins as a listening post, somewhere he could observe as well, and today he had had the opportunity for both. What he had observed had been Mr. Robert Seneschal: indeed he had had some difficulty in avoiding a *tête-à-tête* with him in the library. Seneschal had suggested it with more than common urgency but Russell had ducked smoothly. For one thing he remembered that Seneschal owed him a luncheon, and that he hadn't proposed. Seneschal, Russell considered, was more than a little mean, and his manner hadn't suggested that a chat would be a cosy one.

In fact it had been tense and strained. Russell, eating alone, had watched Seneschal across the dining-room. He was eating his usual meal—potted shrimps, cold beef and salad, though not with pickles since his digestion was suspect, and a half pint of beer drunk slowly. Except for the half pint drunk slowly. Today he was drinking brandy and soda, and Russell, who had excellent eyesight, had noticed that there wasn't much soda. He counted four brandies, and three other men at Seneschal's table. That again was unusual since Seneschal wasn't gregarious. But today he was positively matey; he was trying to be pleasant and much too hard. Russell detested Seneschal, but he wasn't without sympathy, and what he felt now was pity. A politician mending his fences, looking for support where previously he would have snubbed it wasn't a pretty sight. And as Russell left the Mandarins he saw that Seneschal had his *tête-à-tête* after all. Colonel Clarence-Smith had nobbled him and that could mean only one thing. Clarence-Smith was neither politician nor official but his position was known and accepted. He was the Prime Minister's senior hatchet man. Seneschal was under pressure, most likely over Mecron, and Mecron touched Russell too.

Back in his office he settled deliberately, conscious that he had done everything possible, conscious that it wasn't enough. For an official yes, but not for a man who hated Mecron. The stuff was a corruptive drug. Russell hadn't been quite sure the word existed and had looked it up in a dictionary. . . . Yes, a corruptive drug. And there were other words too, the whole language of the junky and of those who tried to cope with him—jargon about the needle, withdrawal symptoms, stabilized addicts. To Russell the last was the most frightening of all. It meant a normal life except for reliance on a doctor's weekly prescription. A normal life! Mecron was supposed to be something between a tranquillizer and a pep pill. You took it and went to sleep; you woke to a febrile activity. You woke to addiction.

An unquiet sleep indeed.

Charles Russell grunted. This wouldn't do at all. Private disapproval, a personal fear, weren't substitutes for action, and to action he saw no door. He began to check it over. Hugh Latta was dead, so the Templeton inquiry would be an honest one: Mecron would be a dangerous drug, and that would take care of the future, of any attempt at import or at clandestine manufacture in the country. Or to be accurate Chief Superintendent Pell would. Russell had the highest opinion of him.

It was the interim which troubled him since he had assumed responsibility for it. And assumed, he thought impatiently, was just about the word. For he hadn't been effective. There had been Mecron in the black market and he had told Rachel Borrodaile to discover where it came from. Presumably she hadn't—no, it was better than a presumption. Rachel Borrodaile was a reliable senior officer, the sort you gave *carte blanche* to. If she'd had anything to tell him she'd have done so. That went without saying.

Nevertheless his hand was on the telephone to ring her when he dropped it. He wasn't a civil servant: it wasn't his habit to give instructions, then stand in a subordinate's shadow, crossing the Ts, pestering him, showing mistrust when the worst was disappointment. On the contrary he valued his reputation as a good delegator. He was rising sixty, too. At sixty, one had to watch oneself; one really mustn't fuss.

He looked at the telephone again, then shook his head decidedly. Put at the highest, emotion aside, the black market had had some Mecron. But they couldn't have had much of it. Perhaps it had just run out, perhaps the supply had quietly dried. In any case Rachel Borrodaile would still be working on it. These things took time and he mustn't be unreasonable.

Unreasonable or not Charles Russell frowned. He would have given a great deal to know what was happening in black market Mecron.

For that he had to wait a while but not for news which shook him. His secretary came in silently, announcing a call by Chief Superintendent Pell. Harold Pell was without appointment but Russell didn't hesitate. His relations with Pell were excellent, far beyond the need for protocol. The frontier between their empires was often vague—vague but observed meticulously. They liked each other personally. Russell wouldn't have dreamt of keeping Pell waiting.

'Good evening, sir.'

Chief Superintendent Pell called Russell sir just twice in every interview, once when it started and once at the end. It precisely defined a friendship which both enjoyed and valued.

'I'm very glad to see you. Please sit down.' Russell poured sherry and Pell accepted. He was a man in his late fifties, tall, dressed in immaculate mufti. He had a long lean face, the actor's mobile mouth, and in private life he was an amateur actor of distinction. He sat in Russell's armchair looking like an intelligent and slightly sardonic horse, an experienced old horse which had seen everything from owners who kept you in training because it was good for their social prestige to jockeys who pulled your head off. He drank some sherry appreciatively, then said easily: 'I've called about something called Mecron. You've no doubt heard of it. Yes? Then I'll be glad when this Templeton inquiry is over. Then I'll know where I am. The Division I try to run can do nothing with a dangerous drug which isn't officially dangerous, far less illegal to handle.'

'I'll be relieved when it's over too. Then I can chuck my hand in. And you can pick it up for us.'

'That's really very frank of you. May I take it you've an interest in Mecron? A *present* interest?'

'When I start lying to policemen I'll be cleverer than I think I am.'

'I'll take that one to pieces sometime. Not that I'm suggesting the slightest impropriety.' Harold Pell waved a graceful hand. 'Quite the contrary. When people like me are hamstrung, not even able to start, it wouldn't surprise me if the Executive showed an interest. You have resources which a vulgar policeman hasn't.'

'We've vulgar resources which a policeman hasn't.'

'That's another I'll have to think about. But just for the moment it isn't a question of what would or wouldn't surprise me but of what I know. I *know* you've an interest in Mecron, though perhaps I couldn't prove it. Not that I need to. Your people have been asking us about a certain organization, and later they borrowed the papers on a man we believe is its leader. If that doesn't point to Mecron I'm a very bad guesser.'

'You're not a bad guesser. There's Mecron in the black market, or rather there was. But I dare say you knew that too.'

'I did. And I was helpless.'

'And in practice I didn't do better, though I've an entirely unprofessional feeling about Mecron. I hate and fear narcotics and I knew that you had your hands tied. I thought that if we could find out where it came from the peculiar resources which you mentioned, our particular advantages. . . .' Russell went eloquently silent.

'I know just how you felt for I often feel the same,' Pell added without irony: 'I'm grateful for your help.'

'But you really mustn't mock me. I totally failed. I don't know where this black market Mecron came from, and maybe I never shall.' Russell looked up suddenly. 'I suppose you're not making a fool of us? I suppose you don't know yourself?'

'No. I dare say we could have discovered if they'd told us to press the buttons, but you know that they didn't.' Harold Pell shrugged. 'But I do know something about Mecron which might interest you.'

'Yes?'

'There's a curious sort of timing, a kind of pattern about it. Our Cypriots had some Mecron, then it seems to have run dry. Nothing was dealt in for several days. Then unexpectedly they had some more.'

'I don't like that at all.'

'No more do I, but I've some sort of comfort for you—what I came to tell you, really. The Templeton will be reporting soon, much sooner than expected.' Pell moved an eyelid lightly. 'I've a friend in the Templeton.'

Charles Russell smiled. 'I accept you've a friend in the Templeton.' The smile disappeared. 'They'll report the right way?'

'Oh yes, it's dangerous all right, but it isn't as simple as that. I don't understand the ins and outs but in layman's language some of it's a habit-forming drug, some of it isn't. They assure me that could happen, and from Hassertons' point of view quite innocently. It's a pretty complicated product. I'm not a chemist, but I don't suppose all the Mecron ever made was made at one sitting. Change the processing of this, your supplier of that, and things could go wrong. As it happens they have—quite unexpected things, quite unforeseen. Whatever your checks, and Hassertons would be scrupulous. . . .' Harold Pell waved a hand again. 'As I say, the technicalities aren't for me, and we'll hear the details

151

later, the scientists' abracadabra. But the fact has been established that Mecron isn't uniform. That's the Templeton's
finding and I trust the Templeton.'

'And so do I.'

Chief Superintendent Pell said softly: 'You mean you do
now.'

Russell sat up sharply. 'Implying I didn't once?'

'Implying just that.'

'Shoot it,' Charles Russell said.

For answer Pell felt in his pocket. He produced a leather
bow, putting it on Russell's desk. He didn't comment for he
was an accomplished amateur actor.

'And what in hell is that?'

'It's the bow from a woman's shoe. The police found it in
Dr. Latta's room the night he met with a misfortune. They
checked on it of course, but they weren't particularly excited.
Finding part of a woman's shoe in a bachelor's apartment
doesn't change what on evidence is an accident into anything
else. So the Divisional police weren't much interested at the
time. They only got excited when they found whom it
belonged to. Then they brought it to me and I think they
did rightly. Now I'm bringing it to you.'

'But why?'

Pell nodded at the leather bow. 'Beautiful thing, isn't it?
Hand made, of course. Look at that stitching. There aren't
more than a dozen shoemakers in London who can still do
work like that. That's how they traced it. That bow is part of
a craftsman's job. It was the shop in Adam Street and it
doesn't have so many women customers.'

There was a long silence while Russell considered the bow.
At last he said simply: 'Thank you.'

'Not at all. I just thought you should know, sir.' On the
sir Harold Pell rose easily, walking to the door. At it he
said: 'A delightful woman, isn't she? A charmer. I wonder
she's never married.' He paused, timing his line perfectly.

'Naturally we don't suggest she murdered him.'

17

THAT EVENING HENRY Leggatt was walking back to Dorset Square from a session at the house in Regent's Park. He was feeling in very good heart. For one thing the instructor had been gently complimentary, and that didn't happen often. And for another, equally unexpected, he had run into Michael East. In the war they had been very close indeed.

They had slipped into a pub for the beer which both thought earned, picking the threads up easily. Michael East was a man whom Henry respected and felt at home with. He was fifty perhaps, but in splendid shape. His background was family business, one which he had built up after the war into a prosperous solidity. He talked about it unaffectedly, with the gusto of a man who loved his work. Henry, he supposed, liked politics.

Henry said flatly he didn't. Not now.

Murmuring something about putting on the weight again they'd just been losing Michael East bought more beer. He settled to listen; he was good at it. When Henry had finished he said: 'You're at a cross roads of course. It's no business of mine, you can tell me to mind my own, but we've been in some spots together. You've quite a lot of life left. You might as well use it.'

'I was thinking like that myself.'

'What'll you do if you chuck politics?'

'I'll sell things again.'

'You mean it?'

'Why not? It's what I really do. I was a director of Hassertons, but that was a title of courtesy. I was really the head salesman.'

'You wouldn't start again as a director.'

'I know it. That's part of the decision.'

Michael East reflected. 'Have you any languages?'

'Pretty fair French. It's rusty now, but it was serviceable once.'

'Would a job in France interest you? Don't get me wrong. I'm not hiring an ex-M.P., far less an ex-Minister. I'm interested in a salesman in the crudest sense. We've not much turnover in France, no branch yet. That would be up to you.'

'You're serious?'

'Perfectly.' Michael East scribbled on a visiting card. 'Ring me there and in forty-eight hours. I said I was serious.'

Henry Leggatt walked back to his flat in an excitement he wasn't concealing. You did get a break—just sometimes. He knew Michael East. East didn't make easy promises nor rat on those he did. Henry Leggatt had a job, a challenge.

He went into the flat, lighting the gas stove. The room was cold but it wasn't lonely. That was something which surprised him. He'd lived with a woman for a good many years and the later ones hadn't been happy. She'd taken a lover and finally sold him shamelessly. Nevertheless plain physical proximity could have left its mark of habit. Henry wouldn't have been astonished if he'd felt a little lonely. Instead he felt simply relieved. And there was something else as well, a hint of apprehension. Patricia had been due back yesterday from Lord Egham's Durham fastness. The train had been timed in London at a quarter to ten, and at a quarter past Henry was mixing a drink which he would have admitted was celebratory. But one day's absence wasn't certainty. She could have been delayed perhaps, she could walk in this evening, she still had her key. . . .

The thought appalled him. He wouldn't know what to do with her.

He sat down at the desk, writing a letter of resignation. He knew there was a form for it, a precedent long established. You cleared it first, then wrote how much you'd enjoyed the association, kind colleagues and fruitful labours. What you got back was equal blah. Henry couldn't pass the lie. He didn't bother with a draft, writing steadily and plainly. He had decided to leave politics; he'd be applying for the Hundreds as soon as it was convenient; meanwhile he was resigning as a Minister. For a moment he was tempted to add something about there being little difficulty in finding a successor, but this wasn't the moment for a barb. He sealed the letter and found a stamp. Then he went out to post it. He'd ring Michael East tomorrow.

When he returned there was a parcel. He saw that it hadn't been posted, simply dropped on the mat through the letter slit. He opened it curiously. Inside the wrapping was a layer of greased paper, and inside the paper two clips of thirty-eight calibre ammunition.

He smiled but uncertainly. Rachel Borrodaile, like East, was reliable: when she said she'd do a thing she did, and reliability was something he could use. He was grateful but also sceptical. For what was he supposed to do? Wave a gun at Dick Asher the next time he called, even fire it if Asher got violent? He supposed that did happen; it happened in the Executive maybe, to the people they never talked about, professionals. But not to himself. English judges had a complex about firearms. Deep in the misty subconscious of the English bench was the conviction that firearms were inherently immoral. You could get a stiffer sentence for firing one, even for keeping it without a licence, than you did for beating a dog to death. Perhaps it was the instinct for survival. Old men, over-privileged, living apart, reality the final enemy. . . .

Henry put the bullets away in a drawer of his desk with his gun. But he did not load it. Straightening he looked from the window. It had been a casual glance, but he went back to his armchair frowning. On the other side of the street two men had been staring into the open bonnet of a car. A tool-kit had been spread on a fender, but neither man had the air of mechanical competence. Whatever the job was it didn't seem urgent. Perhaps they were waiting for help. One of the men had partly turned and Henry had seen his profile. It wasn't Dick Asher but it was astonishingly like him.

Henry went to the window again, despising himself. The other man had turned completely now. He was staring up at Henry's flat and, as he saw him, he swung away suddenly. He had been powerfully built, and dark, not English.

Henry sat down at the desk. . . . After all she had told him to ring her, given him a special number. He valued that more highly than a firearm.

. . . Two men with a broken-down car, not hurrying to mend it, two dark men, Cypriots. . . .

He hesitated but finally picked up the telephone; he dialled three letters, and when a girl answered gave a number without a name. He could hear another telephone ringing out, and waited. Presently a voice said cautiously: 'Miss Borrodaile's telephone.'

'Isn't she there?'

'She's in conference.'

'A real one?'

'Yes, she's really not here. I'm her secretary. Of course I'll take a message.'

'The name's Henry Leggatt. Ask her to ring me back as soon as she's free. How long do you think—'

'She's with somebody pretty important. It might be ten minutes or it might be an hour. If it's really urgent I could fetch her out.'

'Don't do that. But ask her to telephone immediately.'

Henry looked out of the window again. The car was there still and now there were three men, not two.

Rachel had been with Charles Russell on his urgent summons. At first he hadn't spoken; he stared at the leather bow on his desk, then at Rachel Borrodaile. Her face hadn't changed as she saw it. Russell was thinking what a good officer she was, how much he'd hate to part with her. It looked as though he'd have to: she'd grossly exceeded instructions. If she'd been caught at Latta's the whole Executive would have been compromised, and that was unforgivable in a responsible officer. Yes, he'd have to let her go, but his feelings weren't solely of official loss. He liked Rachel Borrodaile personally—liked and admired her. She was a

156

decorative and charming woman, and in the world of the Security Executive decorative and charming women weren't so common. Or not in the office itself. Russell spoke a little wearily.

'We'll have to go through it formally, I'm afraid. You recognize that bow?'

'I do.'

'It was Chief Superintendent Pell who brought it me. Can you guess where it was found?'

'Since it was Pell who brought it—yes.'

'If you'd care to explain. . . .'

She began to do so, concealing nothing now. She had taken her decision instantly, since only a fool hid detail from a Russell already roused. She told the story fully, simply, leaving only her motive to Russell's guess. But it wasn't her motive he chose to question. Instead he said:

'Forget about Hugh Latta. That was stupid of you, but it isn't so important now. What matters now is what you've just told me, that four of Hassertons' directors had a carton of Mecron each. The first supply the Cypriots got hold of would have come from one of those. And that you didn't tell me at the time?'

She shook her head.

'The second must have come from Henry Leggatt. And that you knew too because he told you. That you suppressed as well.'

'I did.'

'But there's Mecron at the factory still and this Asher has strings on Leggatt. He's been to him once, and blackmail's the short word for it. He's threatened to try again. Accompanied. With friends. Which could be something more than blackmail.'

Rachel said miserably: 'Of course I'll resign. If you'll let me, that is. I'll—'

Russell ignored her. 'But he hasn't in fact been again—alone or otherwise?'

'Not as far as I know. Henry was to tell me if he did.'

'That at least was correct.' Russell was dry but not sarcastic.

He drummed on the desk with spatulate finger pads, staring expressionless at nothing.

Rachel broke the long silence. 'I'll resign,' she said again. 'I'll go to my room and write it out.'

'No.' Russell's vehemence astonished her. 'No—or not yet. I can't decently accept it. I've committed the Executive to something not formally its business, and for motives just as personal as yours. Your own I can guess—I've seen you with Henry Leggatt—and mine were in a sense less reputable. I'm head of the Security Executive and I'm not supposed to have feelings at all. I'm not supposed to hate things, even corruptive drugs.' Russell smiled wryly. 'I'm no better than you are and in some ways worse. I can't with decency accept your resignation. More important, I daren't.'

'Meaning?' she asked.

'Meaning that we're involved still. The Templeton hasn't reported yet, though soon, I think, it will. Meanwhile the police can't take it on—Pell made that clear. What's more there's a crisis coming, a crisis for Leggatt personally. We're in this still, and both of us.'

'Then what should I do?'

He asked a second time: 'This Asher hasn't tried again? Not yet?'

'I told you. Henry was to ring me—'

But Russell had stood up suddenly. 'If I were you I'd be pretty close to Leggatt—right in his shadow.' He held his hand out, taking hers. It wasn't a gesture he made often. 'Good luck,' he said.

'You're a wonderful man to work for. Sometime I'll tell you properly.'

'Not now.'

Back in her room Rachel reached for the telephone. 'Get me Mr. Leggatt, please.' She gave her secretary the number.

'Mr. Henry Leggatt? He telephoned half an hour ago and asked you to ring him back. It sounded pretty urgent.'

'Then please get him urgently.'

Three minutes later the secretary said: 'Nobody's answering. The number's ringing out.'

Rachel sat still for perhaps another minute. Then she went to her safe, unlocking it. She put her Luger in her bag. She didn't carry firearms as a habit. The last time she'd touched a gun had been to show it to a matron in a nursing home in Wimbledon, and that had been as evidence that she was someone to be admitted, a respectable employee of the Security Executive. Astonishingly she was still employed by the Security Executive, but respectable. . . .

She wasn't feeling that. She was in fact frightened and she knew about fear. When you were frightened you were usually something else. And that was desperate.

She shut the safe again and ran to the lift. She went to her car and started it.

She drove to Dorset Square outrageously, swearing, jumping the reds. She was sweating and knew it.

Henry Leggatt had been waiting for the telephone to ring. Instead it was the front door bell. He wasn't ashamed that he peeped through the fanlight before opening. What he saw on his doorstep very much surprised him for it was Mr. Robert Seneschal. Henry opened reluctantly; he wasn't in the mood for Robert Seneschal. Come to think of it he seldom had been.

'I know this is quite unexpected. I know—'

'Come in.'

Henry gave Seneschal a drink. Seneschal wasn't drunk but Henry could see that this wasn't his first drink of the evening. Seneschal lowered it quickly, accepting another; he was on edge, something more than nervous, but he seemed to be collecting himself. At last he said portentously, a little owlish: 'I've come to appeal to you personally. After all we are colleagues. We belong to the same great party. We've a joint responsibility.'

'If it's about Mecron again, I gave you an answer. I won't go to Hassertons, I won't ask for favours.'

Seneschal said awkwardly: 'It's not quite that.'

'No?' Henry was surprised again but waited. This was a

Robert Seneschal he'd never seen. He mistrusted the normal Seneschal but he preferred him to this one. This one, scared stiff, was something between obscene and pitiable. This one, stripped naked, was bare of defences—deference and an established position. This was Robert Seneschal as God had made him. Henry thought it an off-form job.

'No, it's not purely Mecron. I've been thinking about that, thinking deeply.' For a moment there was a flash of the accustomed Seneschal. The unspoken implication was that when Seneschal thought, thought deeply, the conclusion would be inescapable. And inescapably correct. 'After all the basic position about Mecron is that we ourselves arranged for the test by the Templeton. After that shameful story in *The Gong* I would have much preferred that the product had been quietly withdrawn—that would have been much less public, the whole problem would probably have died—but I see your point of view, I really do. So that given that a certain amount of publicity is inevitable, what we must show at bottom is that we have done our duty. And that will need presentation, careful presentation. The Templeton isn't an official laboratory—you know our difficulties about invoking one—but its reputation is unchallenged. And it was we who called it in. We could point to that unquestionably.'

From this rigmarole Henry sorted the essential. Being a Seneschal rigmarole it had been one of omission. Henry said quietly: 'So if Mecron's a dangerous drug you've decided you can ride it after all. But, I suppose, for one thing. My own connection with it.'

'Oh no, not that. Not that at all.' Seneschal had said it much too fast. His face was puffy and he was having difficulty with his hands. 'May I. . . . Do you think I could have a drink?'

Henry Leggatt poured him one and Seneschal gulped at it. For a moment it seemed to steady him. Almost normally he said:

'No, it's not personal, or not to you.' Seneschal finished the whisky. 'It's—it's personal to me. I want you to help me.'

'How?'

It came out in a rush, the long words gone, the elaborate parentheses. For the first time in his life Henry was really understanding Robert Seneschal. It had been some time ago, but once Robert Seneschal had almost been Prime Minister. Which was something the present incumbent hadn't forgotten. And the Prime Minister didn't think well of Seneschal's handling of Mecron: on the contrary he had hinted at interference, rather more than hinted that the matter would have been handled a great deal better by those whose business it formally was. So that riding it, simply riding it, wouldn't be enough. The Prime Minister hadn't forgotten, and he was a practising and practised politician. The long knives were out and in willing hands. And there was something else about Lord Egham. Lord Egham and what he stood for were important.

Henry considered as Seneschal talked on. He was talking compulsively now, repeating himself, but Henry didn't stop him. There was something unsaid still, something Seneschal couldn't quite bring himself to utter. Lord Egham kept on coming up, shudderingly being ducked again. Somehow Lord Egham was the key to this.

Henry asked simply: 'And how does Lord Egham come in?'

'He's behind the Prime Minister. He's never liked me. He doesn't like what I stand for, he—'

'But that's common knowledge.'

In his chair Robert Seneschal's knees were apart, his body bent almost between them. He said to the carpet:

'If Egham would change his mind . . . intervene with the P.M. . . . take the pressure off me.' He forced himself to look at Henry, the effort almost shameful. 'The Eghams,' he said. 'You married one.'

Henry walked to the window. The car was there still and the three men fooling with it.

. . . There was a gun in his desk but that was an absurdity. That sort of thing was in another life.

Henry looked at the telephone but he went back to Seneschal. He was sorry for him but furious. This was a humiliation and humiliations should be private. He wanted no part of Seneschal's. This was an intrusion, mental as well as physical. Henry said sharply: 'I've never met Lord Egham.'

'But your wife has.'

'Yes.'

'If you would talk to her and she to him. . . .'

Henry was embarrassed and not for himself. He hadn't counted with Robert Seneschal; he'd been a stooge and not a favoured one, a convenience to be patronized. Now Seneschal was prostrate and Henry hadn't put him there. It would have been different if he had tried to, something to be savoured in success. Instead it was embarrassing. God, it was embarrassing.

Seneschal was repeating: 'If she could speak to him. . . .'

Henry said brutally, not intending to be brutal: 'My wife has left me.' He wasn't a superstitious man, but speaking he crossed two fingers.

In the shocked silence which followed Henry poured more drinks. His back was to the door but he heard it open. He swung, spilling both whiskies. Three men were advancing.

. . . The key. Patricia had hers still. Patricia had had a key.

The first man struck at him. He rolled with the blow, but he was holding the drinks and was tired. The blackjack caught him but not quite squarely. He fell with the drinks but harder.

He picked himself up slowly, trying not to vomit. Two men were standing over him and one had a knife. The third was beating Seneschal. He had hit him once already and Seneschal was folding. His hands were at his face, his head thrust into them. As he collapsed his neck came forward. The third man hit it once; and once again very quickly.

Somebody said: 'Steady.'

Seneschal fell on his face and the third man rolled him over with his foot. His shoulders moved before his head. The third man had to move that too to look at it.

'You bloody fool. You've killed him.'

The third man bent, loosening Seneschal's coat, his shirt, putting his ear to his heart. 'He's alive,' he said at last. He turned to the room. 'Who is he?'

Nobody answered.

The man with a knife moved it suddenly. Henry moved too, much quicker now, but it had only been a gesture.

'No good. We're three to one. Who is he?'

'He's a friend of mine.'

The man with the knife hesitated, finally shrugged. 'Not that it matters. We can't take him with us, but he won't be moving for at least an hour. And that should be enough . . . for *you*.' He was staring at Henry Leggatt. 'March,' he said crisply; he nodded at Robert Seneschal. 'Unless you want your share of that—a basinful. It hurts. Move, man, and quick.'

'Move where?'

'*We'll* decide that.'

'You'll have to do more than decide.'

The man with a knife smiled, beckoning to the third. The three stood round Henry silently, then knife said something in a language Henry didn't know. The other two nodded, silent still. The man with a knife lowered it slowly, the point still upwards. Henry watched it calmly, for to this he knew the answer. . . . The upwards thrust, the block, the twist and elbow lock, the arm which broke with matchstick ease. He knew the answer. . . .

But not to all of it, not to three men in unison. The knife began to move again and Henry with it. For an instant he was off balance and the second man slid, sweeping his feet from under him. He fell against the knife-arm but the knife had stopped. But the third man hadn't. He still had the black-jack and he hit Henry twice and expertly.

The second man picked himself up, walking to the window, looking at the street. 'It's clear,' he said, 'or as clear as it ever will be. It's women, mostly.'

'Get hold of him, then.' It was knife again. The other two lifted Henry. 'Ready?'

'I don't like that one on the floor. If he dies—'

'If he dies there's a queue for hell.' Knife opened the front door, jerking his head at the waiting car. 'Put Leggatt in the back and stay with him. I'll drive.'

The other two trotted past him, carrying Henry. One of them was laughing. He said to the man with the knife: 'Don't forget your manners, boy. Shut the door behind you.'

18

RACHEL ARRIVED JUST five minutes later. She knocked and rang, then went back to the Giulietta to think savagely. Henry was expecting a call from her, had asked her to ring him urgently, and Dick Asher had been explicit: he'd come again and not alone. Russell had taken that seriously; Russell, instead of sacking her, had told her to act. Rachel took her notebook from her handbag. Dick Asher's address was already in it.

She drove to Pont Street in a mounting fear, ignoring the hall porter, running up the stairs and ringing. A woman opened to her.

'Is Mr. Asher in?'

'I'm afraid he's not.'

Rachel looked at the woman. They'd been casually introduced at a party but Patricia Leggatt hadn't been interested in Rachel Borrodaile. She'd drifted away to company more congenial, but Rachel had the professional's memory for faces. She said shortly: 'Then I want to talk to you.'

'Who are you? What are you selling?'

Rachel pushed past her firmly. She had, when she wished, a cool arrogance the equal of any Egham's. Besides, she was half a Frenchwoman, and to the Frenchwoman the English upper class had been decidedly devalued. Rachel walked into the sitting-room and Patricia followed her. Patricia sat down but didn't invite Rachel to. Rachel took a chair.

'You're Mrs. Henry Leggatt?'

'I am. And who are you?'

'My name's Rachel Borrodaile. I work in the Security Executive.'

But only just, she thought.

'A policewoman?'

'Yes.' The distinction wasn't worth making.

'May I see your card, please.'

Rachel produced it. She opened her bag to do so much wider than was necessary. She could see that its contents hadn't escaped Patricia Leggatt.

'Thank you. And now—'

'I'm looking for Mr. Asher.'

'I told you—he isn't here.'

'I've good reason to believe you. Do you know where he is?'

'I do not.'

Rachel said quietly: 'You're in a frightful jam, you know.'

'I don't know what you mean. You're impertinent, you're—'

Rachel ignored her. 'This isn't your husband's house, but I wasn't referring to that. It's a Mr. Richard Asher's, and Asher is known to the police.'

'Indeed? Then if you know so much about him why are you asking me?' Patricia wasn't scared yet; she said coolly: 'You're bluffing.'

'I never bluff.'

'No? Then I call you.'

Rachel opened her bag again. Part of her was trying not to laugh. This was ridiculous, an outrage. She was Rachel Borrodaile—Security Executive but very much front office. Carrying guns about. . . . All that had been years ago. Waving a gun at the wife of a Minister. . . .

Patricia Leggatt was looking down a well-kept Luger. Rachel said conversationally: 'Observe the silencer.'

'You'd never dare use it. Policewomen don't fire guns.'

'But this is where it's interesting. For you. You see, I know about you too.' Rachel began to talk and Patricia listened Her expression had changed, but she interrupted: 'But none of that's a crime.'

'I didn't say it was. Not yet.'

'Then you're wasting your time.'

'I hadn't quite finished. I know your husband too. You're Henry Leggatt's wife and I'm a policewoman. That's something in common since we're neither of us men. And that's important. I've known Henry Leggatt for a very long time. I knew him before you did and just recently I've known him —well, I've known him pretty well again.'

The Luger moved slightly and Patricia flinched. Rachel Borrodaile noticed it.

'You follow me, I hope.'

'I'll have you dismissed. I'll break you. I'll—'

'The key of your husband's flat, please. Quick.' The gun came up slowly, the safety catch clicking. There was a second of hesitation, then:

'I haven't got it.'

'Why?'

'I gave it away.'

'To whom?'

'I gave it to Dick Asher.'

'When?'

'An hour ago.'

In the silence an electric clock ticked fatly. The tension was insupportable: one of them must break and it wouldn't be Rachel. The gun didn't move but Patricia did. She cracked quite suddenly, dropping her head in her hands. Rachel rose, standing over her.

'Where's Richard Asher?'

'He isn't here—I swear it.'

'For once I can believe you. Where could he have gone?'

'They've a little place in Camden Town, a grocer's in Albert Street. He took me once when nobody else was there. You go through the shop, upstairs. . . .'

But Rachel was at the telephone. She was holding the gun with one hand, dialling with the other. She was dialling a nursing home in Wimbledon. A Cockney voice answered cagily:

'St. Justine's nursing home. Top floor.'

'Charlie? Charlie Lightlove? Rachel Borrodaile here.'

'Why, Miss Rachel.'

'Charlie, will you help me? I'm afraid it's out of school.'

'Of course I will.'

'It's pretty irregular.'

'Good.'

'I'm at a flat in Pont Street.' She gave him the address. 'Collect me here. The job's in Camden Town and probably it's a rough one.'

'Should I bring a gun?'

'I've got one, I'm using it now. On a woman. Silly. . . . Have you got the address right?'

Lightlove read it back again. 'And Miss Rachel, I've company here, a chap called Ted. He's a learner but a game one. Should I bring him along?'

'I've a job for Ted too. Looking after a lady, the one I'm waving firearms at. Charlie, I feel a fool. . . . And Charlie—'

'Ma'am?'

'Step on it for Christ's sake.'

'We'll step on it.'

Rachel went back to her chair. Through the talk on the telephone Patricia had been sobbing. Once broken she had reacted in near-hysteria, but now she was recovering. She took some time but Rachel waited. She was thinking that she'd have to wait in any case. It would be thirty minutes from Wimbledon, even with Charlie's foot down and better than average traffic, and, through central London, fifteen more to Camden Town at best. Forty-five minutes, three quarters of an hour. In three quarters of an hour Henry Leggatt. . . .

Her free hand stiffened.

Presently Patricia spoke again: 'Would you care for a drink?'

'Not with you.'

'May I get one myself?'

'Where is it?'

Patricia pointed. 'There—in the corner.'

'Walk slowly to the corner and mix yourself a drink. Put a foot out of line and it's the last drink you'll pour. I'd be glad of the excuse.'

Patricia came back with a large neat whisky, drinking it greedily. It seemed to be biting. Rachel Borrodaile watched her. She hated her bowels but that was personal. Just for the moment Patricia was something at gun-point, something that could still be tiresome. Patricia Leggatt had still to be disposed of. Rachel said impersonally:

'You couldn't have thought you'd get away with this.'

Patricia finished the whisky. 'Dick Asher,' she said, 'he—'

'You're going to say he led you.' Rachel was contemptuous. 'The man-thing tempted me.'

'But that's just what he did. You said we were women, both of us: you ought to understand. He tempted me all right.'

'You've a husband though one mightn't think so.'

'Dick Asher's going to marry me.'

'*What?*'

. . . How stupid could a worldly woman be, how far be blind?

'He's flying to Nice tomorrow—we're to meet there. I've been here two days, I've burnt my boats, and I was leaving tonight from Heathrow. He gave me the ticket, I've got it here.' Patricia made an unconscious movement towards her bag.

'Keep still.'

'But I'm only trying to convince you. Dick gave me his promise and the ticket. A little money too till he arrived. He came in an hour ago with a man I didn't know, a rough. I gave him the key and he gave me the ticket. The two were . . . went together.'

'Did he tell you why he wanted it?'

'No.'

'I don't believe you.'

'But you must. I wondered why he wanted it myself. You seem to know about Mecron so I can talk about that. There's no Mecron in our flat—not now.'

Rachel said grimly: 'Your husband was probably there.'

'I didn't think. I—'

But Rachel let it pass. 'Did Asher say anything about the place in Camden Town? Tonight?'

'He didn't mention it.'

'He wouldn't. Just the same you gave your husband's latchkey to Dick Asher and a rough. You know something about Dick Asher—not everything perhaps, but more than enough. You know he has an interest in Mecron because you sold him some. So he comes to you with a gorilla and you give him your husband's key.'

'I told you . . . I've burnt my boats. . . . We were to meet in Nice tomorrow.'

'For God's sake be quiet.' Rachel was feeling sick but she was thinking. Patricia Leggatt was an embarrassment, or at least for the next few hours. She might use the telephone and very inconveniently. Rachel couldn't take her with her—manpower couldn't run to it—and tying people up, locking them in bathrooms. . . .

It would be shockingly amateurish, not Executive at all.

Patricia had begun to weep again, twisting her fingers. She wasn't a type which crying suited; her face was ravaged, pitiable, but Rachel felt no pity. What she felt now was horror. She was almost frightened of Patricia Leggatt. . . . A lovely face and behind it a sewer. Henry hadn't meant a thing to her, not even decency, Henry who at this moment . . .

Rachel looked quickly at the electric clock.

Ten minutes to wait still.

Patricia was saying through her handkerchief: 'Let me go—I must meet him in Nice. I *must*. I can't go back to Henry now.'

For the first time Rachel lost control. She had forgotten about the Security Executive. The relief was considerable.

'You bitch. . . .'

But Rachel recovered quickly. Her bow was ironical. 'A breach of discipline,' she said. 'Not the first, but you wouldn't know that. I suppose I should apologize. I don't.'

The front door bell rang urgently and Rachel rose. She backed to the door, opening it behind her, stepping away from it. Lightlove and another man came in. The other man shut the door. Both saw the pistol and neither crossed it. They stood to one side and Lightlove said politely: 'We trod on it —you told us.' He looked round the room. 'And what goes on? By the way, this is Ted.'

170

Ted clicked his heels.

'Charlie, you come with me. Ted, the piece with the crying act is Mrs. Henry Leggatt. Not that it matters. Take her to London Airport and put her on the evening flight to Nice. There's one about midnight and a ticket in her bag. She's not to use the telephone nor speak to anyone unnecessarily. She'll go with you very willingly, but she's not to *talk*. You understand?'

Ted clicked again. 'But perfectly.'

'You came in a car, of course?'

'We did.'

'Then use the one you came in. I'll go with Charlie in mine.'

Ted turned to Patricia Leggatt. 'At your service,' he said. 'Your luggage?'

'There's a suitcase on the chair there.'

Ted picked it up and they walked past Rachel. She was putting the gun away, not looking at Patricia. For the first and last time she was feeling almost sorry for Patricia. Patricia Leggatt had it coming—plenty at that.

Rachel and Charlie Lightlove ran to the Giulietta. Charlie could drive beautifully but didn't offer to; he sat in silence as Rachel explained the background quickly, her eyes never leaving the road. She was talking fast and driving a great deal faster. She ended with the immediate job in hand.

'So the odds are they've snatched Henry Leggatt. It might be as a hostage, but more likely it's for information about the factory. He was once a director and he'll still know the basic lay-out. They'll want him to talk and they're capable of making him.'

'I've noticed you're not dawdling. But this place in Camden Town, this hideaway—how do we get in?'

'I haven't a plan but I do have a gun. Charlie, I've got to tell you this. I'm pretty desperate; I'm in this personally, and you know what that might mean. If you'd like to change your mind—'

'Why, Miss Rachel.' Charlie was offended. He thought for a minute as the car raced on, then said: 'I gather it's a room above a shop.' He glanced at his watch. 'It's barely eight o'clock and in Camden Town they *work*. If the shop's still open it might be easy. We'd walk into the shop itself and crash the rest. There'll be only the inside doors.'

'We'll pray for that.'

'Miss Rachel?'

'Yes.'

'If you'd like me to take the gun. . . .'

'I would not. If there's that sort of trouble it's mine.'

Charlie didn't speak again till Rachel stopped in Albert Street. She was out of the car before him, running into the open shop. There were two women serving still; a handful of customers; and instant silence. Rachel looked round, pointing at a narrow door.

'Where does that lead to?'

A second's hesitation, then: 'Upstairs.'

Charlie went to the door, feeling the handle. The door was locked. He took from his pocket a piece of steel, perhaps a foot long. One end was flattened deeply. Charlie put the flat end in the jamb, pulling on the other gently, working the broad end in. When he was satisfied he pulled again, much harder. There was a splintering crack. 'Old-fashioned,' Charlie said. 'Corn, really, but it works.' He pushed the door open, glancing at the shattered lock. 'Very poor wood.'

They ran up the stairs, Rachel leading. Behind them in the shop a woman had started screaming. Charlie said briefly: 'I saw a telephone.'

'I don't mind the police, I'd welcome them. I want five minutes first, though.'

They were on a little landing now, three doors leading off it. Behind one of them there was a stifled noise. It might have been a groan.

Charlie, very quietly, tried the door. 'It's open. I'll go in first.'

'You won't. I've got the gun.'

Lightlove shrugged. 'There's a chance they'll simply rush

us. If that happens keep together. Grab a corner and watch for knives.'

He threw the door suddenly and Rachel went in. The room held five men. Dick Asher she recognized from photographs but the other three she didn't. The fifth man was Henry Leggatt. He was naked to the waist, tied to a chair under a single electric light bulb. Henry was unconscious.

Four men were looking at a silenced Luger. It wasn't pointing at any one man. That was something they noticed for they knew about guns.

'Weapons in the fireplace—quick.'

There was a tinkle as a knife fell in the grate. A cosh went after it, and something which made Rachel flush. The Luger turned deliberately on to the last, bald man.

'You. Throw it down.'

'I'm clean.'

'We'll see.'

Charlie fanned the fourth man neatly, producing a gun, balancing it with approval. 'But very, very stupid. If you thought you could draw before an angry woman got you. . . .' He began to laugh quietly.

'Now up against the wall, all four of you.' It was Rachel again. 'Two guns against nothing, but hands behind your necks.'

They lined up silently.

'Charlie, you cover them. I'll untie Leggatt.'

'Keep them covered yourself while I check this gun.' Charlie did so expertly. 'Okay, now I've got them.'

Rachel moved to Henry Leggatt. Straps held him and she freed them. He slid slowly to the floor.

She stood over him, for the first time uncertain, but the movement had brought him to. He began to rise deliberately, first hands and knees, then on his haunches, finally upright. Rachel had to help him.

'Harry, what's happened?' She tried to sit him down again but he shook his head; he moved shakily to the fireplace, leaning against the mantel, breathing deeply. 'Is there a drink?'

One of the men against the wall began to move.

'Keep still, damn your eyes.'

The man stepped back again, pointing. Rachel went to a cupboard and found brandy. She brought it to Henry and he drank it grimacing. 'Cypriot stuff. It tastes of petrol. We had it in the war, and it poisoned more men than the Gestapo.' He was recovering slowly.

'Harry, you need an ambulance.'

'As it happens I don't, or not just yet. Tomorrow I won't be able to move, but for the present I can. It was the strap, a rubber strap. Pretty professional, but nothing to what happened once. It hurts at the time but it's later it really gets you. Tomorrow I'll be rigid—horrible—but for an hour. . . . Give me a cigarette.'

Rachel gave him a cigarette. The room was very quiet. Henry smoked most of the cigarette, then threw the stub away. He was looking at the bald man and Rachel at Henry Leggatt. He was shaken still but, stripped to the waist, impressive. There was fat on him still but there was muscle too. He looked a formidable male animal and he was staring at the bald man. 'Baldie,' he said, 'come here.' His voice was very soft.

The bald man didn't move.

Henry spoke to Charlie. 'You with the gun. I'll have to thank you sometime, but for the moment let the bald one go. Cut him out from the others.'

'Get into the middle. Move.'

The bald man walked into the middle of the room, his hands behind his head still.

'All right. Put your hands down.'

The bald man did so, staring in turn at Leggatt. 'And now?' he said. He was a bully but not a coward.

'Now I want to talk to you. And hard.'

The bald man rushed him suddenly, striking savagely, wickedly low. Henry didn't seem to move much—a trip, a push which looked almost gentle. He had taken two paces away from the fireplace, seven or eight feet perhaps, and for Baldie they were dreadful feet. He pitched across them helplessly, arms and legs flailing, not even able to protect his head.

He smashed into the fireplace, cursing, spitting teeth. Two smears of blood were drooling from the corners of his mouth, the caricature of a Manchu's moustache.

He picked himself up slowly and now he had the knife. Rachel's gun began to move again but Henry spoke first.

'Don't fire. I'll settle this.'

He settled it very quickly, quicker than Rachel could follow. She saw the knife come up, the block, a sudden twist. There was a sound she had heard before, the sickening sharp crack of human bone. A scream. Another quick turn by Henry. For the first time he was exerting himself, using his strength and not the bald man's. The bald man was across his hip and then, in a parabola, he wasn't. He was across the room, lying against the door, inert. The crash came an instant later.

Rachel, bright-eyed, was looking at Henry, jerking her head towards Dick Asher against the wall. She heard herself say incredibly: 'And that one—what's for him?'

But Henry laughed. 'I haven't a thing against him. We've been having a little chat in the intervals of Baldie's fun and games. It was intended to break me finally—the psychological touch, you know—and it was about where my wife was living. Instead Mr. Asher has done me a favour; he's simplified everything beautifully. I wouldn't lay a finger on him. Once I would have taken him apart quite happily. Not now.' Henry looked at Dick Asher almost amiably. 'Thank you,' he said.

In the silence which followed there was a knock at the door. Rachel opened it six inches; she looked outside and nodded. 'Push,' she said brightly. 'Push pretty hard. There's a body against it.'

A sergeant of police came in, two constables behind him. The middle-aged sergeant looked round the room.

'Well, well, well.'

Rachel was watching the sergeant. The fatuous patter of the music hall policeman didn't deceive her. Shrewd eyes were sweeping the room, behind them experience working. . . . This had been a gang fight. There were weapons in the fireplace, parked there, no doubt, on some gentleman's agreement, and a man in his trousers whom they'd probably been beating. And something had gone wrong: somehow the gentleman's agreement hadn't been so gentlemanly. There was a man with a gun still and three against a wall. A fourth who looked dead but probably wasn't. . . . Just an ordinary Cypriot gang fight.

Except for one thing, or rather a woman. Cypriots were careful of their women, they seldom involved them, and in any case this woman hadn't quite the air. . . .

The sergeant pointed at Rachel's pistol, asking the routine question:

'Have you a licence for that?'

'Oddly enough I have.'

The sergeant looked surprised. Rachel's manner, not her answer, had surprised him.

'Have you got it with you, ma'am?'

'I have.' Rachel produced the licence and the sergeant examined it.

'Miss Rachel Borrodaile?'

'Yes. But please turn it over.'

The sergeant did so, his expression changing again.

'I see,' he said finally. 'Or rather I don't. I take it perhaps I *needn't*.' He nodded at Charlie Lightlove. 'That chap with the other gun—he's one of yours too?'

'He is.'

'Well, I'm only the station sergeant but we've a very nice telephone. I expect you'll want to use it when we get there.'

'You're very obliging.'

'That man on the floor—he isn't dead, I hope. If he's dead it's going to be much more awkward. For us, I mean. For you, I dare say, too.'

'I don't think he's dead.'

'I'm glad. Killings get too complicated—too many people interested. You follow me, Miss? But of course you do. And now if you'll put those guns away. . . .'

176

19

CHARLES RUSSELL AND Chief Superintendent Pell were in Russell's room next morning. Both were reading copies of *The Gong* and both were smiling. Both had good reason to since *The Gong*'s front page was a relief to each of them. The temptations of a first-class story to professional writers-up of first-class stories had been very much stronger than a trifle like continuity. Mecron was mentioned, but only as a drug which a disgraceful gang of Cypriots had been trying to hijack from the factory which made it. *The Gong* disapproved of foreigners—it was one of the things which sold it—and it had always hated Cypriots. . . . How long would a supine government tolerate this scandal? By a constitutional accident Cypriots weren't aliens; they could enter the country without so much as by-your-leave and, when they got here, what did they do?

This was what they did, and worse.

It was a very much stronger story, much more attractive than any suggestion that Mecron itself mightn't be all it seemed to be. *The Gong* wrote it simply, straight, and with enormous competence; it didn't blur its line by looking backwards. There had been a splash about Mecron a bare fortnight before: it might never have been printed. Mecron, today, was simply what these criminals had been trying to steal. There wasn't a word of comment on the drug itself. For this was a story—hard—and *The Gong* knew its readers.

Charles Russell chuckled greyly. 'They've been kind to our Leggatt too,' he said.

'Of course they have. Leggatt's a hero—the ex-director kidnapped and tortured, holding out and rescued. A fortnight ago there was a suggestion that he was a corrupt politician covering up a product which he knew was dangerous—a scoundrel. But you can't run both lines together, and last night he was a hero. So you have to kill the scoundrel.' Harold Pell chuckled. 'It's elementary editing.'

'You'd have made a good journalist.'

'Perhaps.'

'Not that it's going to matter much to Leggatt—not as a politician. He's resigned as a Minister and he's leaving the House. He's found a respectable job. That isn't yet public but you can take it it's correct. I was told late last night, and it came from the horse's mouth.'

'The horse went straight to hospital.'

'The mare if you insist, then.'

'Miss Borrodaile—ah yes. If I may ask you . . . ?' For once Harold Pell was a little diffident. 'All this reacts on *us*, you know. There were guns on both sides and a considerable rough house. Also a man called Lightlove. I know about Charlie Lightlove—his connection with you, I mean—but it'll be awkward if he's called in court. Perhaps he needn't be—we'll try and fix our lawyer-men, and the accused won't have much motive to want him in the box. But Miss Borrodaile we can't avoid.'

'I know. She's lost her use to the Executive. I've seen her once this morning and I'm seeing her again at noon. I'm not looking forward to it.'

'We'll keep what we can out of court. I'm afraid it can't be everything.'

'I'm much obliged. I am indeed.'

The Chief Superintendent shrugged. 'My turn tomorrow, and you'd do the same for me. She's a very brave woman, anyway. Be kind to her.'

'As gentle as I dare.'

'I leave that side to you, of course. But I wanted to be sure we had it straight between us—what I can do and what I can't.' Pell's manner changed briskly. 'So now I've some news for you, and I don't think you'll have had this bit before me. For once I'd even bet on it since Asher only started talking a couple of hours ago. But when he broke he broke. They mostly

178

do. He told us about Mecron—everything. It seems to fit all right. Our Cypriots were trying to make Mecron themselves. They never doubted it was a habit-former—they'd seen what some of it did—and once it was declared so they'd have smuggled it in or tried to. They wouldn't have brought in all of it, but you know the business much too well to believe we could have netted everything. Odd parcels would have slipped through, and with the sort of people it was going to, not known or recognized addicts, that would have set us a stiffish examination. But now we don't have to pass it. For one thing we hold the leaders, and we can put them away for years. Comforting thought, that. Charges of assorted mayhem even if we never mention drugs. It isn't quite impossible we won't —we'll see. And even more important, there won't be any Mecron for Asher and friends to trade in.'

'You sound very sure of it.'

'I am. You remember I told you about the Templeton's discovery—that some of Mecron's dangerous, some of it isn't?'

'I do indeed.'

'Well, the boys have had the same experience. They keep a tame chemist called Rikky and he was trying to manufacture Mecron for them. He made a good deal of it, but he only produced the sort that's quite innocuous. Naturally, I've told the Templeton. They were pretty excited. They've a man flying off this morning, since this Rikky could help them. His failure could confirm their own experiments. There's something in Mecron with a name a yard long, and the Templeton's conclusion is that it's more unstable than was known. That was their word, not mine. It's quite a fashionable chemical too: plenty of other drugs contain it. I'm not suggesting that the whole of the pharmacopœia will have to be taken to pieces, but it's a fact that Mecron isn't the only product which is going to need looking at.'

'Lucky for Hassertons. Also for the politicos.' Charles Russell smiled his most mordant smile. 'I was thinking politically. I'm supposed to, you know.'

'I hope you're supposed to explain.'

'To you, of course. Taking Hassertons first, Hassertons were up against it, weren't they? Once it came out in Parliament that the Templeton was working on Mecron, Hassertons were committed to it. They couldn't just scotch it—not a firm of that standing. They hadn't an option and now they have again. They're not actively at fault: the worst you could say against them is that they've been using something which has more than one known reaction. That's layman's language but the scientists will go to tcwn on it. They'll have to at that, since you tell me that Hassertons weren't by any means the only people using this something. But the one thing they'll try to avoid—officials and politicians too—will be public disquiet about some chemical in more or less common use. If I were Sir Herbert Hasserton I'd be a much-relieved man. He's still in a bit of trouble but he isn't alone. On the contrary it's to everybody's interest to pull him out quietly. Quietly—that's the operative word again.'

'The velvet glove, in fact.'

'Velvet my foot. The fine old-fashioned smother. They're still extremely good at it.'

Harold Pell laughed. 'Hassertons have been lucky—yes. But what about our political masters? Suppose *The Gong* beats again.'

'Ah. . . . But if I were a Minister I'd be reckoning to muffle it.' Russell picked one of two copies of *The Gong* from the wastebasket, spreading it on the desk again, looking at it distastefully. 'Suppose they went back to the old line. That'd be difficult after running Leggatt as a paladin, but we'll accept that *The Gong* might do anything. So what do they go for? *Who* do they go for? Leggatt's resigned, and he timed it remarkably neatly, though he couldn't have realized it. With the Templeton report still unpublished even *The Gong* couldn't say he'd resigned because of it, and if they talked about advance and unauthorized knowledge, hinted at rats and the sinking ship, I should think it would cost the earth. Too expensive a libel even for *The Gong*. They calculate their risks.'

'But they might not use names at all; they might simply

attack Mecron again. Or Her Majesty's Opposition might.'

'I concede that *The Gong* might. In theory. It isn't *Gong* form, though. They much prefer smearing people and abstractions don't sell newspapers. And as for the Opposition, if I were a Minister with the Templeton finding in my pocket I wouldn't feel too frightened if it went for me. Charge me with failure of duty over Mecron and I'd simply deny it. Moreover I'd turn the tables. I'd look smug as a beneficed priest, something politicians don't find difficult. Leggatt's connection with Hassertons was dangerous, but Leggatt has gone and perfectly honourably—flags flying, guns firing. Or rather, thank God, not firing. Which leaves the plain fact that it was a Minister who first invoked the Templeton. Is that alone so promising for a rampant Opposition. How right the good Minister was!'

Chief Superintendent Pell considered it, finally smiling. 'We'll keep our fingers crossed.' He rose with his actor's timing. 'So everybody's happy, more or less. The Executive's happy because it's out of Mecron. I'm happy because, though I'm in it now in principle, Mecron won't plague me in practice since there won't in fact be any. Henry Leggatt's out of politics and into a job he wants. Ministers have an answer if they need one, all the more effective now that Leggatt isn't one of them. So everybody's happy. . . . Yes?'

'Except Robert Seneschal.'

Harold Pell sat down again; he said softly: 'Since you mention him—'

'But I haven't a story; I'd share if I had. I know no more than you do.' Russell said 'know' with a familiar precision. 'A senior Minister was calling on his junior at his private house. No doubt they were discussing some routine ploy, some squalid political swindle but a perfectly normal one.'

'You really think that?'

'It's all I *need* to think. And that Seneschal chose his calling time very unfortunately. For Seneschal. How is he, by the way?'

'He's still unconscious with a fractured skull. The doctors say he'll live with luck, but he'll never again be Seneschal.'

The Chief Superintendent rose for the second time. At the door he couldn't resist his exit line again. He bowed politely, the irony judged cannily. 'Thank you for your co-operation, sir.'

Russell didn't rise to it. 'At your service,' he said. 'As always.'

Harold Pell went out but Russell didn't move. He was frowning abstractedly. It wasn't quite true that everybody was happy except Robert Seneschal. There was a Mrs. Henry Leggatt too. Russell hadn't felt obliged to pass to Pell what Rachel had told him of Patricia Leggatt. She was out of the country, anyway; she'd hardly come back just yet—perhaps not at all. He wondered where she'd live, and how.

Poor, horrible, finished woman.

Russell's frown deepened. And there was himself as well: he wasn't too happy either. He looked at the clock. In half an hour he was seeing Rachel Borrodaile again and he couldn't stall for ever. Hell! He was in it himself still whatever the ending. Miss Borrodaile had to be disciplined and he couldn't himself do it. He was head of the Security Executive but he wasn't yet a hypocrite.

Damnation take Mecron, the pit all politics. In half an hour he was seeing Rachel Borrodaile and he didn't know what to say to her.

Robert Seneschal woke about noon in a room he didn't recognize. It had the spare, inhuman cleanliness of the high-class clinic, and his wife was talking quietly to a nurse in uniform. He opened his eyes and shut them again. He wasn't yet in pain but instinct warned him that very soon he might be. Consciousness recovered wouldn't be wholly a blessing. He peeped at the women again, obscurely deciding that he wasn't yet ready for them. He wasn't yet ready for anything. He couldn't move his head.

He heard someone stir, and for a moment a hand was on his forehead, cool as the little room. He supposed it was his wife's but he didn't feel moved to look at her. There was a murmur of women's voices, impersonal in its detachment, and a door shut softly. He was alone with the nurse.

He came to again much later, still with a nurse but another. The curtains were drawn now, but he sensed that it was dark outside. The lighting was very dim. Seneschal lay for five minutes, fighting a mounting pain, watching the nurse. She was knitting intently and hadn't yet noticed that he was conscious. When she did she would send for a doctor and the doctor would give him morphia. Robert Seneschal knew that, for he'd twice had operations. He used the interim to think, aware that he couldn't think clearly. Half of his mind seemed to work, the other half wouldn't. He could remember a man with a stick—not really a stick—a shattering agony at the base of his skull, a second blow almost merciful. . . . And what had he been doing—where? It had been something to do with politics but he couldn't remember what. Politicians didn't strike you, or not with sticks. Politicians had other weapons.

He tried to shrug and failed. For an instant it didn't register, then panic seized him brutally. A shrug was the simplest reflex and the reflex hadn't functioned. He lay in a primal terror. His right arm wouldn't move at all: it didn't hurt him but nor did it obey. He tried the left, inching the hand up under the blanket, watching the nurse still, feeling his neck, his head. There was plaster and something cold like steel.

Very slowly he worked his hand back again. He couldn't remember and didn't desire to. That part of him wasn't working, but another was alive again. Seneschal wished it wasn't.

He thought about the future . . . God, but he didn't have one. Six months it would be and maybe more. And two would be enough. Two months away from politics was two months too many, even if the Prime Minister had been friendly. They couldn't leave a ministry vacant for six months, not even Social Welfare, and when you came back again, if you came back again. . . .

Robert Seneschal was too old a hand to delude himself. He

hadn't made many friends, and certainly the Prime Minister wasn't amongst their number. The Prime Minister wouldn't hesitate; he'd seize his chance and gratefully. Once and for all.

Seneschal saw that the nurse's eyes were on him. She rose at once and pressed a bell, coming to the bedside, smiling at him coolly.

'How do you feel?'

'Not very well.' His voice surprised him for it wasn't above a whisper.

The nurse looked at her watch. 'It's half past six. Your wife will be here at seven.'

His wife, he thought—Helen, Consort to Robert Seneschal Esquire, Privy Councillor and a senior Minister. Now an ex-Minister, a broken-down backbencher, nobody. He'd never climb back for they'd never let him.

. . . Back to the Senior Common Room? But he was much too old. Some sinecure in business, then? But the business world mistrusted him. Robert Seneschal was finished.

Well, he could always farm again. If Helen would still pay for it.

By mid afternoon Patricia Leggatt had stopped crying. The foreign edition of *The Gong* had arrived at noon, and she had seen it in her *pension* in Nice. It had told her in six sentences that Dick Asher wouldn't be joining her. Then, half an hour later, they had called her to the telephone. That had surprised her, but it hadn't been Dick Asher's voice. It had been a cold voice, calmly minatory, and the message had been unequivocal. She was to keep her mouth shut, not to talk to anybody—but anybody. . . . Understood? And she wasn't to come back to England.

Well, she remembered, she couldn't. She wasn't perhaps a criminal but she'd been very near to crime. She knew much too much for comfort. Sometime maybe. . . .

This year, next year, sometime, never. She couldn't go back to Henry—Henry and that woman Borrodaile. Henry had

184

motive now, and competent lawyers. Whether or not they found her they'd go for a divorce. And she couldn't defend an action. She'd openly stayed at Dick Asher's, since it hadn't then mattered. She hadn't a leg to stand on.

And precious little else. She began to count her money. There wasn't a great deal of it for Dick Asher had been joining her. That voice might send her some or more likely it would not. It hadn't been a kind voice and she'd no weapon against its owner. Who didn't have to bribe her to keep her out of England. She had a little money of her own but it wasn't in France. It wasn't easy to bring income out of England unless you could show illness, and for Patricia Leggatt it might even be too dangerous to try. She spoke fair French, enough to find a menial job in a country which wasn't fussy. But she wasn't a Frenchwoman; she hadn't a permit to work, and she knew what that did to wages. If she went to the consul he'd have read the papers too; he'd recognize her name, start wondering, asking questions. At the lowest she was an important witness, conceivably a good deal more. And there was always that voice. She was a stranger in a foreign land, a penniless refugee.

That was something she had read about.

She looked round the room. It was clean but it wasn't grand. Soon, she knew, very soon, she'd be remembering it as luxury.

Rachel Borrodaile walked into Russell's room at noon; she walked lightly, gaily, her limp almost unnoticeable, and for a moment Russell felt something which was almost irritation. Damn the woman, she shouldn't be so cheerful. And she looked about twenty. He expressed his annoyance as he had been trained to, indirectly. He looked at her feet.

'New shoes, I see.'

It didn't even prick her. 'Oh that. I've come to save you trouble about that.' Rachel put an envelope on the desk. 'That's my resignation.'

'I told you I couldn't ask for it.'

'You haven't.'

'I'm not even sure I'm going to accept it.'

'It's perfectly freely offered.'

'You say.'

'I mean. Look, I can't run a house and work for you. Much as I adore you.'

'What's this about a house?'

'We're taking one.'

'We?'

'Yes.'

'He's a fortunate man, that Leggatt. Where are you going to live?'

'In France—for a bit at any rate. Henry's got a job there, and I've got bits and pieces.'

'You've money in France too?' Russell seemed surprised.

'I've—well, I've assets. After the war I left quite a bit behind me. Remember I'm half French, and I've a wholly French contempt for anything like exchange control. I've never quite trusted a British government.'

'How right you've been.' Russell poured sherry reflectively. 'You must ask me to the wedding.' He watched her drink the wine in silence. 'Well?'

For a moment she was almost shy.

'I haven't asked him yet.'

unquietsleep00hagg

(Continued from front flap)

strange reports began to filter into London's Security Executive about this supposedly harmless tranquilizer. Discreet investigation uncovered highly placed connections with the matter.

A fascinating puzzle is skillfully revealed and solved here by an expert in this sort of behind-the-scene machinations where the acquisition and retention of power leads to desperate measures.

Jacket design by Bob Ritter

IVES WASHBURN, Inc.

New York